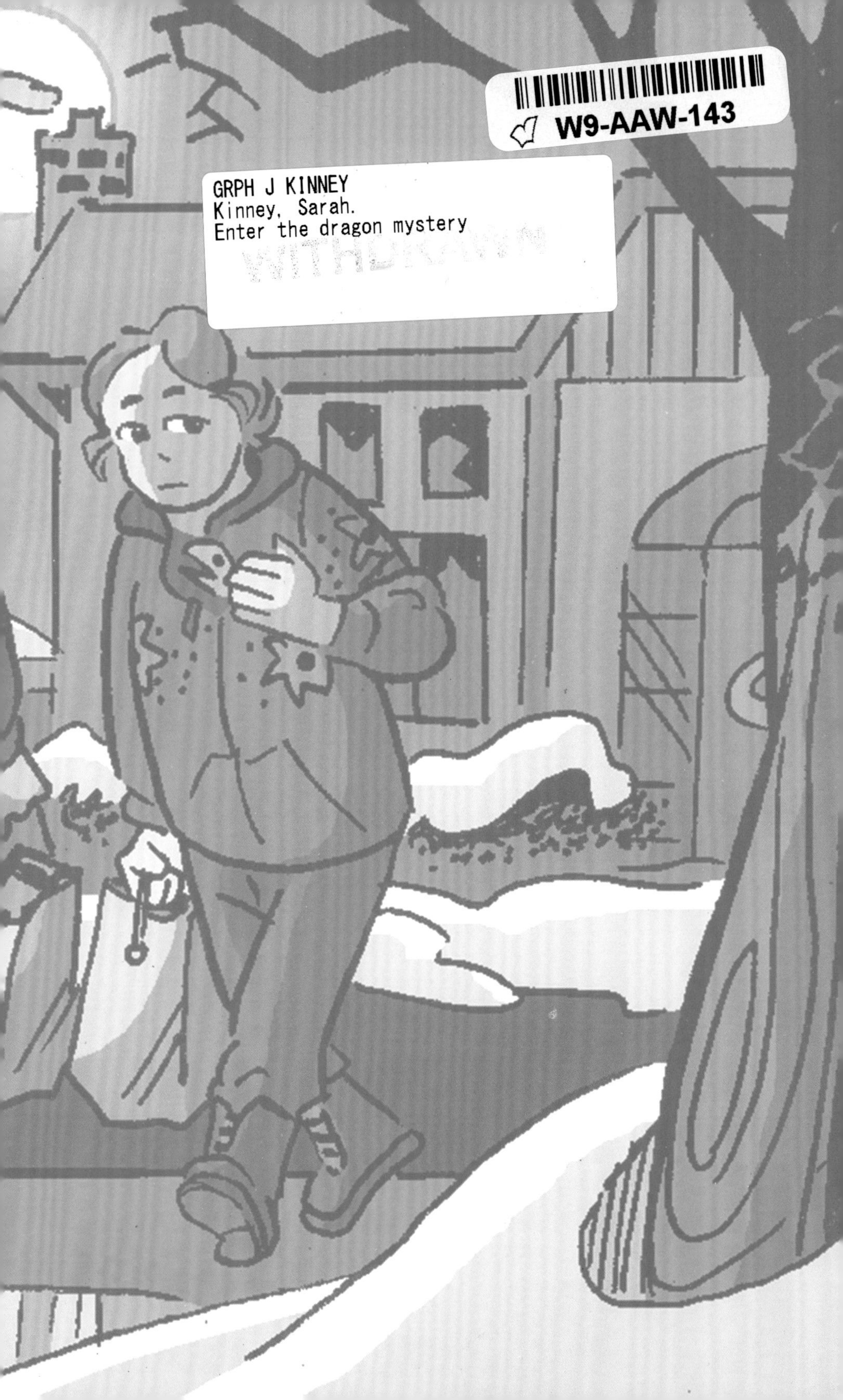

NANCY DREW AND THE CLUE CREW®

"MY CLUE CREW AND I ARE WILLING TO DO WHATEVER IT TAKES TO BRING THAT EVILDOER TO JUSTICE."
- NANCY DREW

PAPERCUTZ™

NANCY DREW GRAPHIC NOVELS AVAILABLE FROM PAPERCUTZ

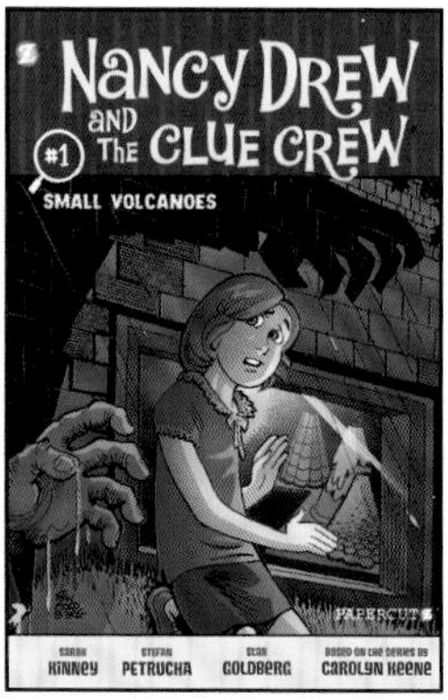
Nancy Drew and the Clue Crew
#1
SMALL VOLCANOES
PAPERCUTZ
SARAH KINNEY
STEFAN PETRUCHA
STAN GOLDBERG
BASED ON THE SERIES BY CAROLYN KEENE

NANCY DREW AND THE CLUE CREW #1
"Small Volcanoes"

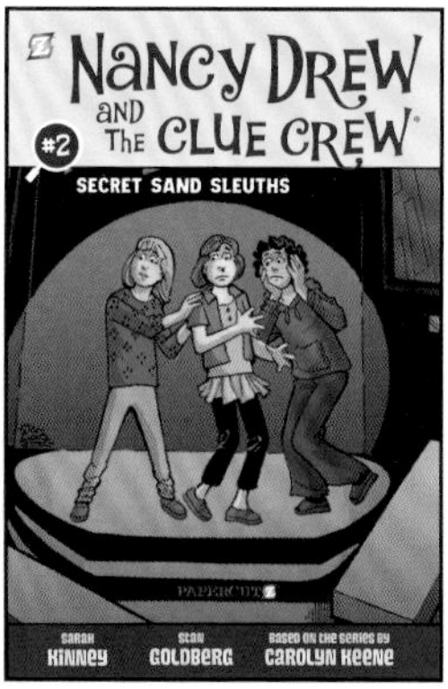
Nancy Drew and the Clue Crew
#2
SECRET SAND SLEUTHS
PAPERCUTZ
SARAH KINNEY
STAN GOLDBERG
BASED ON THE SERIES BY CAROLYN KEENE

NANCY DREW AND THE CLUE CREW #2
"Secret Sand Sleuths"

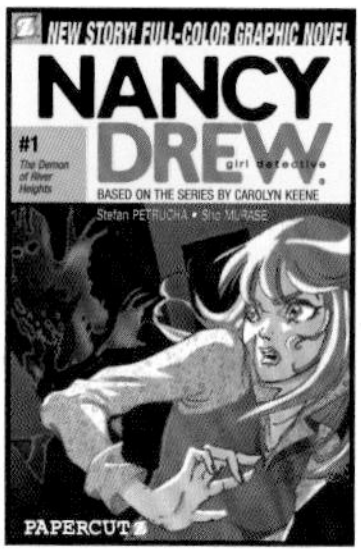
NEW STORY! FULL-COLOR GRAPHIC NOVEL
NANCY DREW
girl detective
#1
BASED ON THE SERIES BY CAROLYN KEENE
PAPERCUTZ

#1 "The Demon of River Heights"

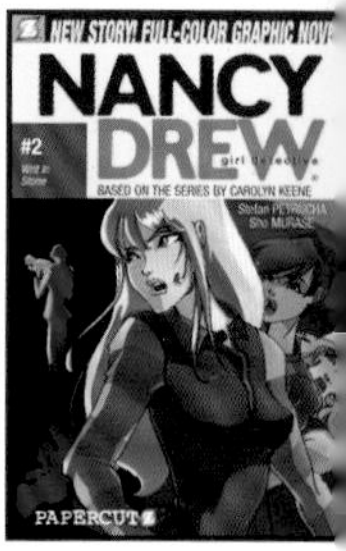
NEW STORY! FULL-COLOR GRAPHIC NOVEL
NANCY DREW
#2
BASED ON THE SERIES BY CAROLYN KEENE
PAPERCUTZ

#2 "Writ In Stone"

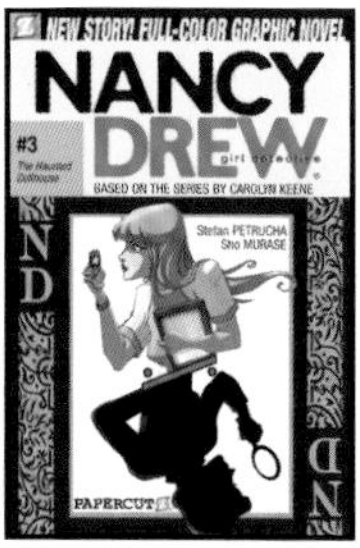
NEW STORY! FULL-COLOR GRAPHIC NOVEL
NANCY DREW
#3
BASED ON THE SERIES BY CAROLYN KEENE
PAPERCUTZ

#3 "The Haunted Dollhouse"

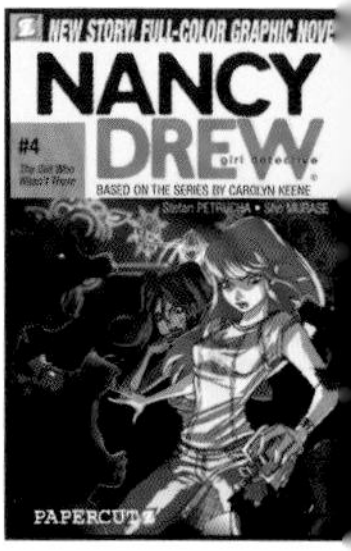
NEW STORY! FULL-COLOR GRAPHIC NOVEL
NANCY DREW
#4
BASED ON THE SERIES BY CAROLYN KEENE
PAPERCUTZ

#4 "The Girl Who Wasn't There"

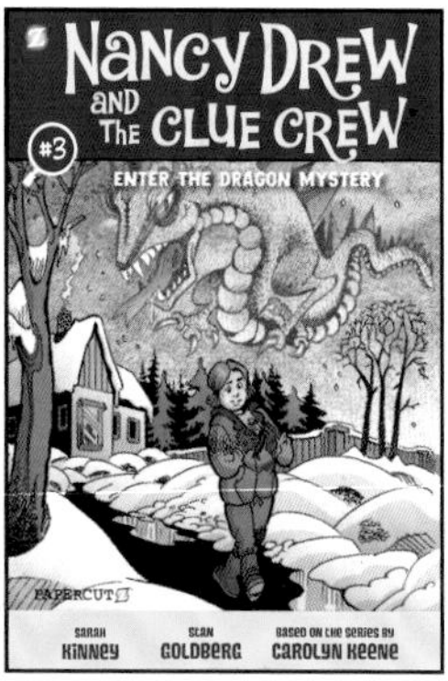
Nancy Drew and the Clue Crew
#3
ENTER THE DRAGON MYSTERY
PAPERCUTZ
SARAH KINNEY
STAN GOLDBERG
BASED ON THE SERIES BY CAROLYN KEENE

NANCY DREW AND THE CLUE CREW #3
"Enter the Dragon Mystery"

COMING SOON!

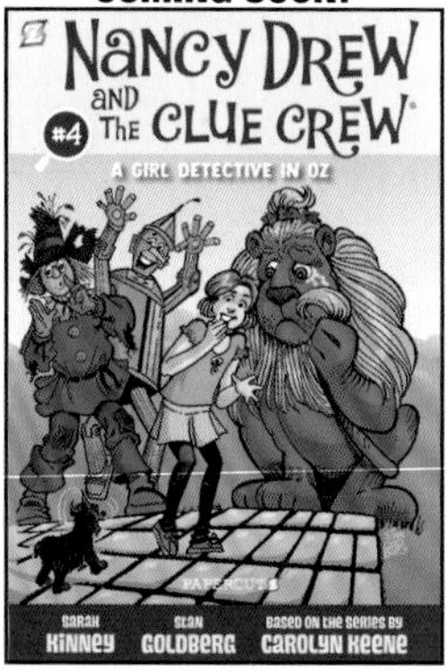
Nancy Drew and the Clue Crew
#4
A GIRL DETECTIVE IN OZ
PAPERCUTZ
SARAH KINNEY
STAN GOLDBERG
BASED ON THE SERIES BY CAROLYN KEENE

NANCY DREW AND THE CLUE CREW #4
"A Girl Detective in Oz"

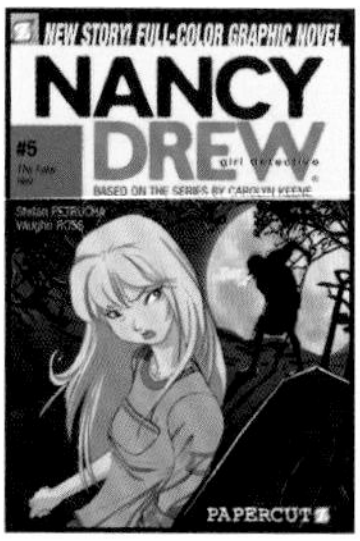
NEW STORY! FULL-COLOR GRAPHIC NOVEL
NANCY DREW
#5
BASED ON THE SERIES BY CAROLYN KEENE
PAPERCUTZ

#5 "The Fake Heir"

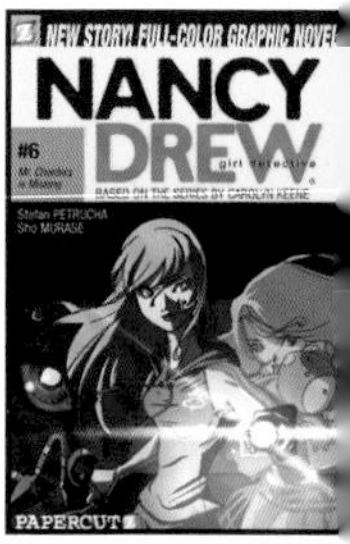
NEW STORY! FULL-COLOR GRAPHIC NOVEL
NANCY DREW
#6
PAPERCUTZ

#6 "Mr. Cheeters Is Missing"

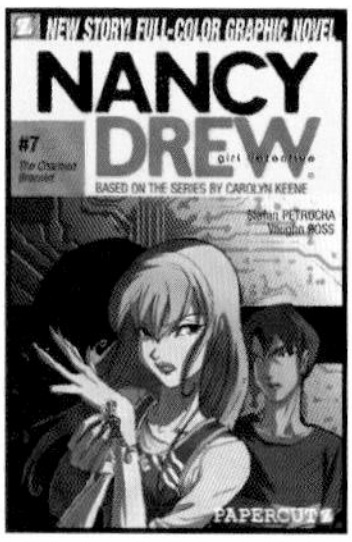
NEW STORY! FULL-COLOR GRAPHIC NOVEL
NANCY DREW
#7
BASED ON THE SERIES BY CAROLYN KEENE
PAPERCUTZ

#7 "The Charmed Bracelet"

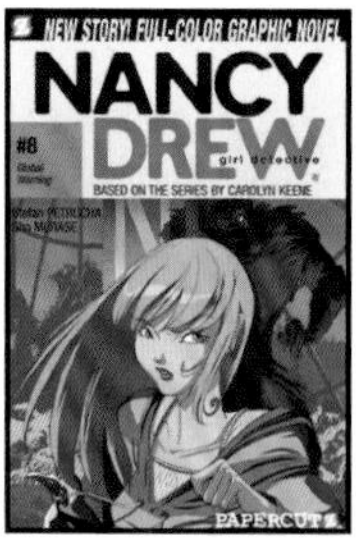
NEW STORY! FULL-COLOR GRAPHIC NOVEL
NANCY DREW
#8
BASED ON THE SERIES BY CAROLYN KEENE
PAPERCUTZ

#8 "Global Warning"

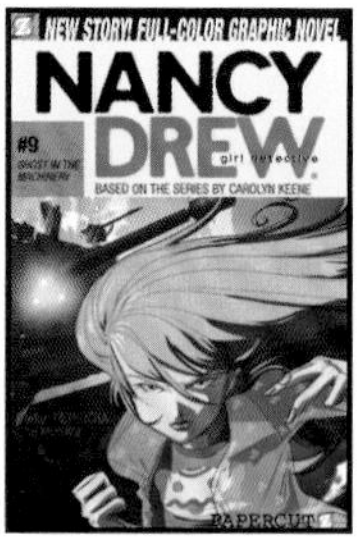
NEW STORY! FULL-COLOR GRAPHIC NOVEL
NANCY DREW
#9
BASED ON THE SERIES BY CAROLYN KEENE
PAPERCUTZ

#9 "Ghost In The Machinery"

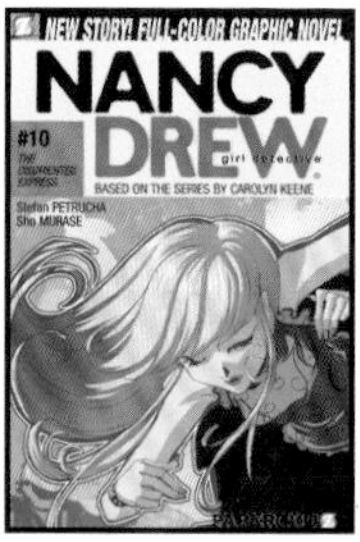
NEW STORY! FULL-COLOR GRAPHIC NOVEL
NANCY DREW
#10
BASED ON THE SERIES BY CAROLYN KEENE
PAPERCUTZ

#10 "The Disoriented Express"

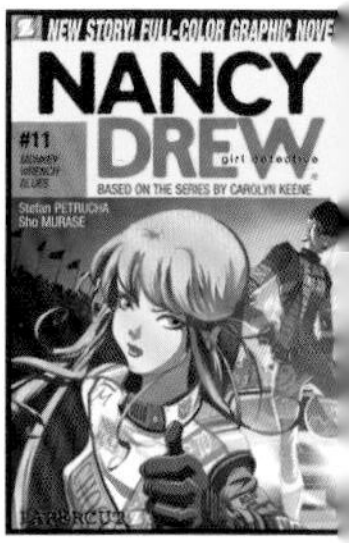
NEW STORY! FULL-COLOR GRAPHIC NOVEL
NANCY DREW
#11
BASED ON THE SERIES BY CAROLYN KEENE
PAPERCUTZ

#11 "Monkey Wrench Blues"

See page 55 for more NANCY DREW graphic novels!

NANCY DREW graphic novels are available at booksellers everywhere.

NANCY DREW graphic novels are $7.95 each in paperback and $12.95 each in hardcover. NANCY DREW AND THE CLUE CREW graphic novels are $7.99 each in paperback, and $11.99 each in hardcover, except #1, which is $6.99 in paperback; $10.99 in hardcover. You can also order online at www.papercutz.com. Or call 1-800-886-1223, Monday through Friday, 9 – 5 EST. MC, Visa, and AmEx accepted. To order by mail, please add $4.00 for postage and handling for first book ordered, $1.00 for each additional book and make check payable to NBM Publishing.
Send to: Papercutz, 160 Broadway, Suite 700, East Wing, New York, NY 10038.

NANCY DREW and NANCY DREW AND THE CLUE CREW graphic novels are also available digitally wherever e-books are sold.

www.papercutz.com

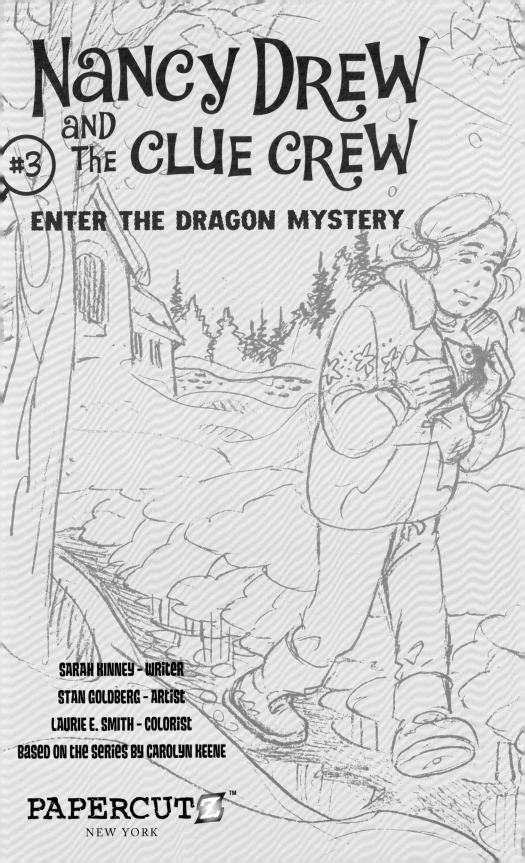

NANCY DREW AND THE CLUE CREW

#3

ENTER THE DRAGON MYSTERY

SARAH KINNEY - WRITER

STAN GOLDBERG - ARTIST

LAURIE E. SMITH - COLORIST

BASED ON THE SERIES BY CAROLYN KEENE

PAPERCUTZ™

NEW YORK

Nancy Drew and the Clue Crew
#3 "Enter the Dragon Mystery"
Sarah Kinney – Writer
Stan Goldberg – Artist
Laurie E. Smith – Colorist
Tom Orzechowski – Letterer
Production – Nelson Design Group, LLC
Beth Scorzato – Production Coordinator
Michael Petranek – Associate Editor
Jim Salicrup
Editor-in-Chief

ISBN: 978-1-59707-437-7 paperback edition
ISBN: 978-1-59707-438-4 hardcover edition

Printed in China
October 2013 by Asia One Printing, LTD
13/F Asia One Tower
8 Fung Yip St., Chaiwan, Hong Kong

Distributed by Macmillan

First Printing

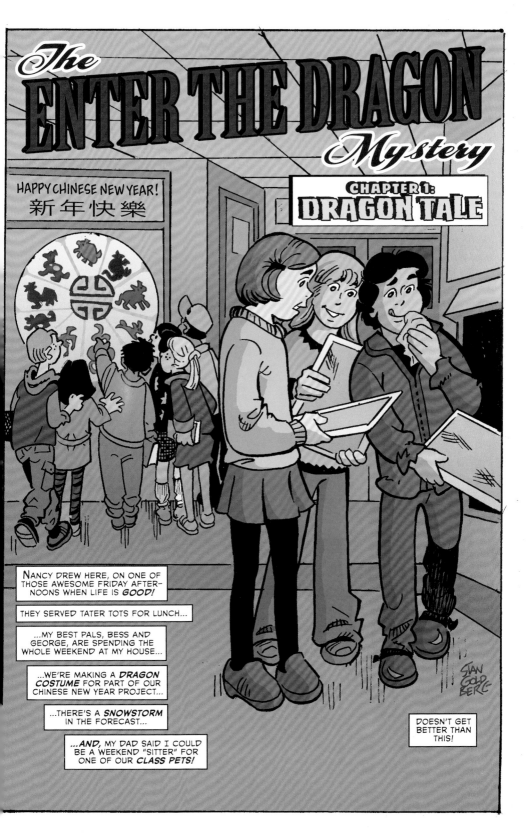

The ENTER THE DRAGON Mystery

HAPPY CHINESE NEW YEAR!
新年快樂

CHAPTER 1: DRAGON TALE

NANCY DREW HERE, ON ONE OF THOSE AWESOME FRIDAY AFTERNOONS WHEN LIFE IS *GOOD!*

THEY SERVED TATER TOTS FOR LUNCH...

...MY BEST PALS, BESS AND GEORGE, ARE SPENDING THE WHOLE WEEKEND AT MY HOUSE...

...WE'RE MAKING A *DRAGON COSTUME* FOR PART OF OUR CHINESE NEW YEAR PROJECT...

...THERE'S A *SNOWSTORM* IN THE FORECAST...

...*AND,* MY DAD SAID I COULD BE A WEEKEND "SITTER" FOR ONE OF OUR *CLASS PETS!*

DOESN'T GET BETTER THAN THIS!

STAN GOLDBERG

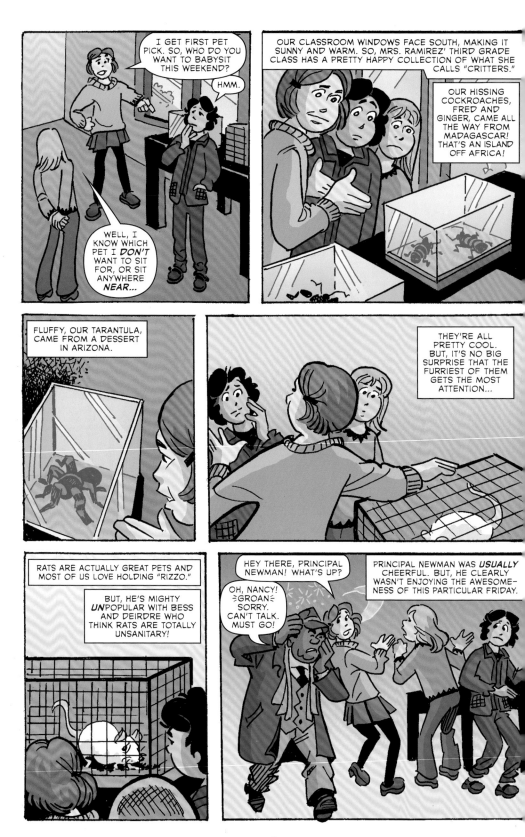

I GET FIRST PET PICK. SO, WHO DO YOU WANT TO BABYSIT THIS WEEKEND?

HMM.

WELL, I KNOW WHICH PET I *DON'T* WANT TO SIT FOR, OR SIT ANYWHERE *NEAR...*

OUR CLASSROOM WINDOWS FACE SOUTH, MAKING IT SUNNY AND WARM. SO, MRS. RAMIREZ' THIRD GRADE CLASS HAS A PRETTY HAPPY COLLECTION OF WHAT SHE CALLS "CRITTERS."

OUR HISSING COCKROACHES, FRED AND GINGER, CAME ALL THE WAY FROM MADAGASCAR! THAT'S AN ISLAND OFF AFRICA!

FLUFFY, OUR TARANTULA, CAME FROM A DESSERT IN ARIZONA.

THEY'RE ALL PRETTY COOL. BUT, IT'S NO BIG SURPRISE THAT THE FURRIEST OF THEM GETS THE MOST ATTENTION...

RATS ARE ACTUALLY GREAT PETS AND MOST OF US LOVE HOLDING "RIZZO."

BUT, HE'S MIGHTY *UN*POPULAR WITH BESS AND DEIRDRE WHO THINK RATS ARE TOTALLY UNSANITARY!

HEY THERE, PRINCIPAL NEWMAN! WHAT'S UP?

OH, NANCY! ⇒GROAN⇐ SORRY. CAN'T TALK. MUST GO!

PRINCIPAL NEWMAN WAS *USUALLY* CHEERFUL. BUT, HE CLEARLY WASN'T ENJOYING THE AWESOME-NESS OF THIS PARTICULAR FRIDAY.

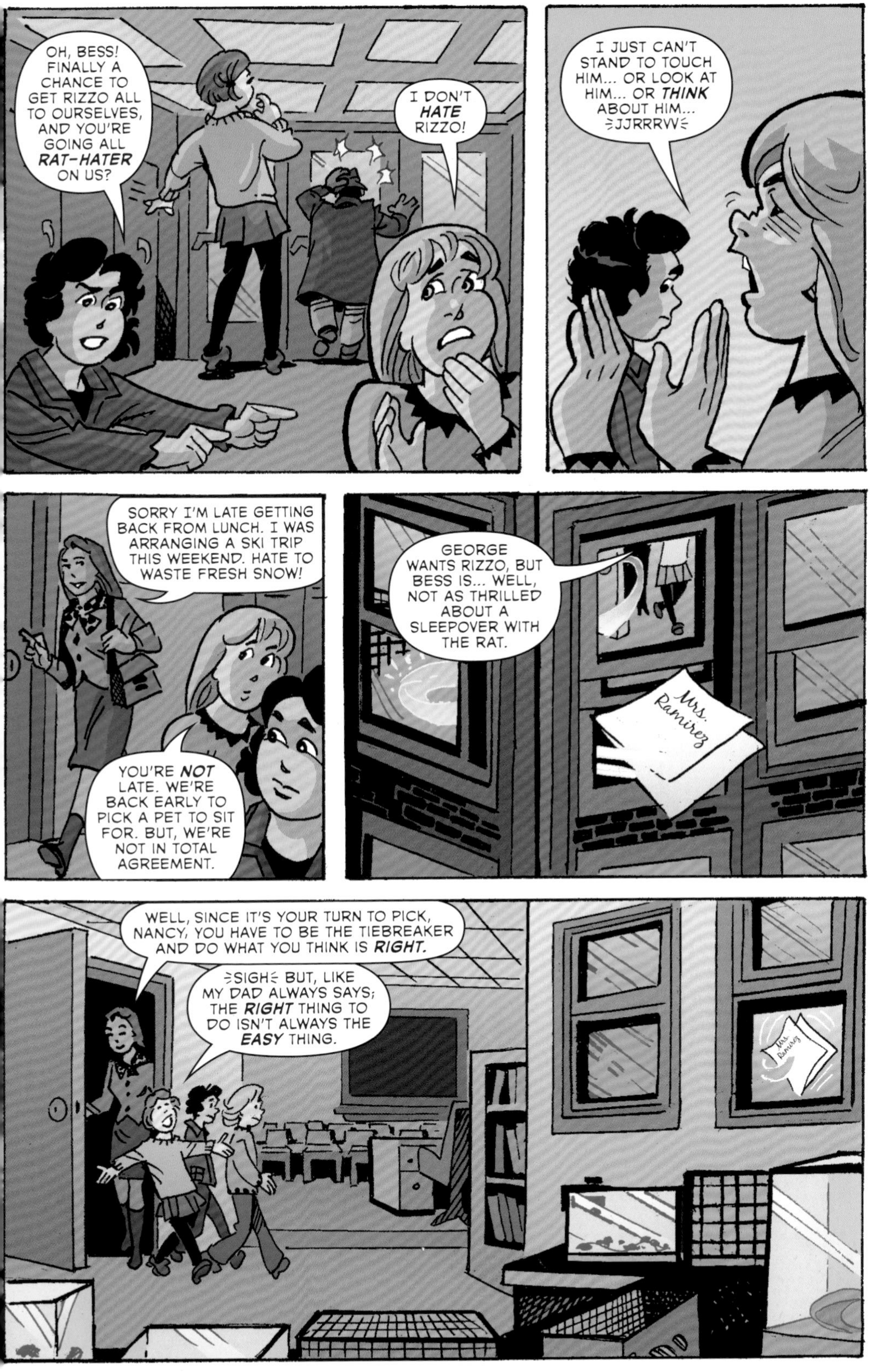
OH, BESS! FINALLY A CHANCE TO GET RIZZO ALL TO OURSELVES, AND YOU'RE GOING ALL RAT-HATER ON US?
I DON'T HATE RIZZO!
I JUST CAN'T STAND TO TOUCH HIM... OR LOOK AT HIM... OR THINK ABOUT HIM... ≷JJRRRVV≶
SORRY I'M LATE GETTING BACK FROM LUNCH. I WAS ARRANGING A SKI TRIP THIS WEEKEND. HATE TO WASTE FRESH SNOW!
YOU'RE NOT LATE. WE'RE BACK EARLY TO PICK A PET TO SIT FOR. BUT, WE'RE NOT IN TOTAL AGREEMENT.
GEORGE WANTS RIZZO, BUT BESS IS... WELL, NOT AS THRILLED ABOUT A SLEEPOVER WITH THE RAT.
Mrs. Ramirez
WELL, SINCE IT'S YOUR TURN TO PICK, NANCY, YOU HAVE TO BE THE TIEBREAKER AND DO WHAT YOU THINK IS RIGHT.
≷SIGH≶ BUT, LIKE MY DAD ALWAYS SAYS; THE RIGHT THING TO DO ISN'T ALWAYS THE EASY THING.
Mrs. Ramirez

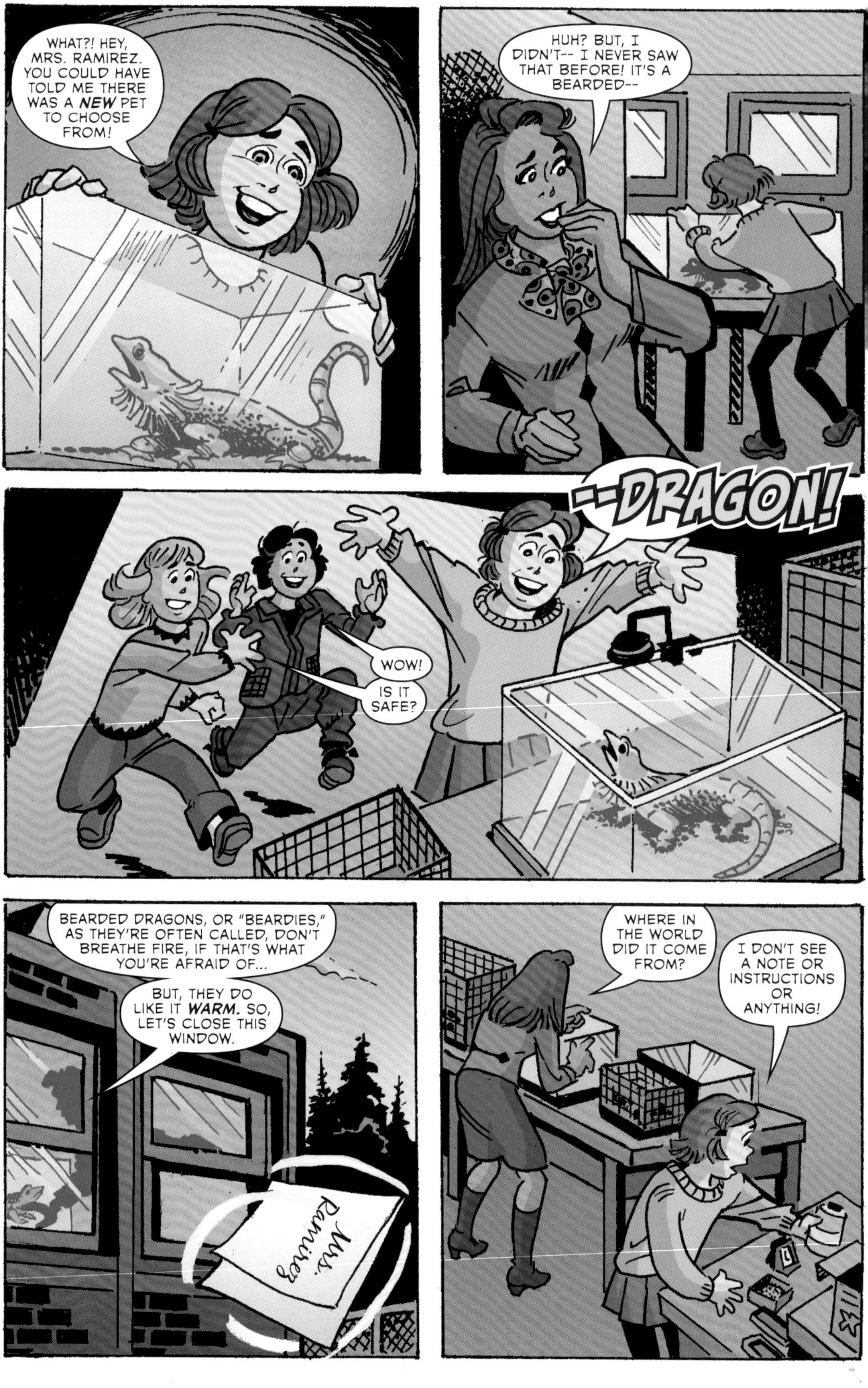
WHAT?! HEY, MRS. RAMIREZ. YOU COULD HAVE TOLD ME THERE WAS A NEW PET TO CHOOSE FROM!
HUH? BUT, I DIDN'T-- I NEVER SAW THAT BEFORE! IT'S A BEARDED--
--DRAGON!
WOW!
IS IT SAFE?
BEARDED DRAGONS, OR "BEARDIES," AS THEY'RE OFTEN CALLED, DON'T BREATHE FIRE, IF THAT'S WHAT YOU'RE AFRAID OF...
BUT, THEY DO LIKE IT WARM. SO, LET'S CLOSE THIS WINDOW.
Mrs. Ramirez
WHERE IN THE WORLD DID IT COME FROM?
I DON'T SEE A NOTE OR INSTRUCTIONS OR ANYTHING!

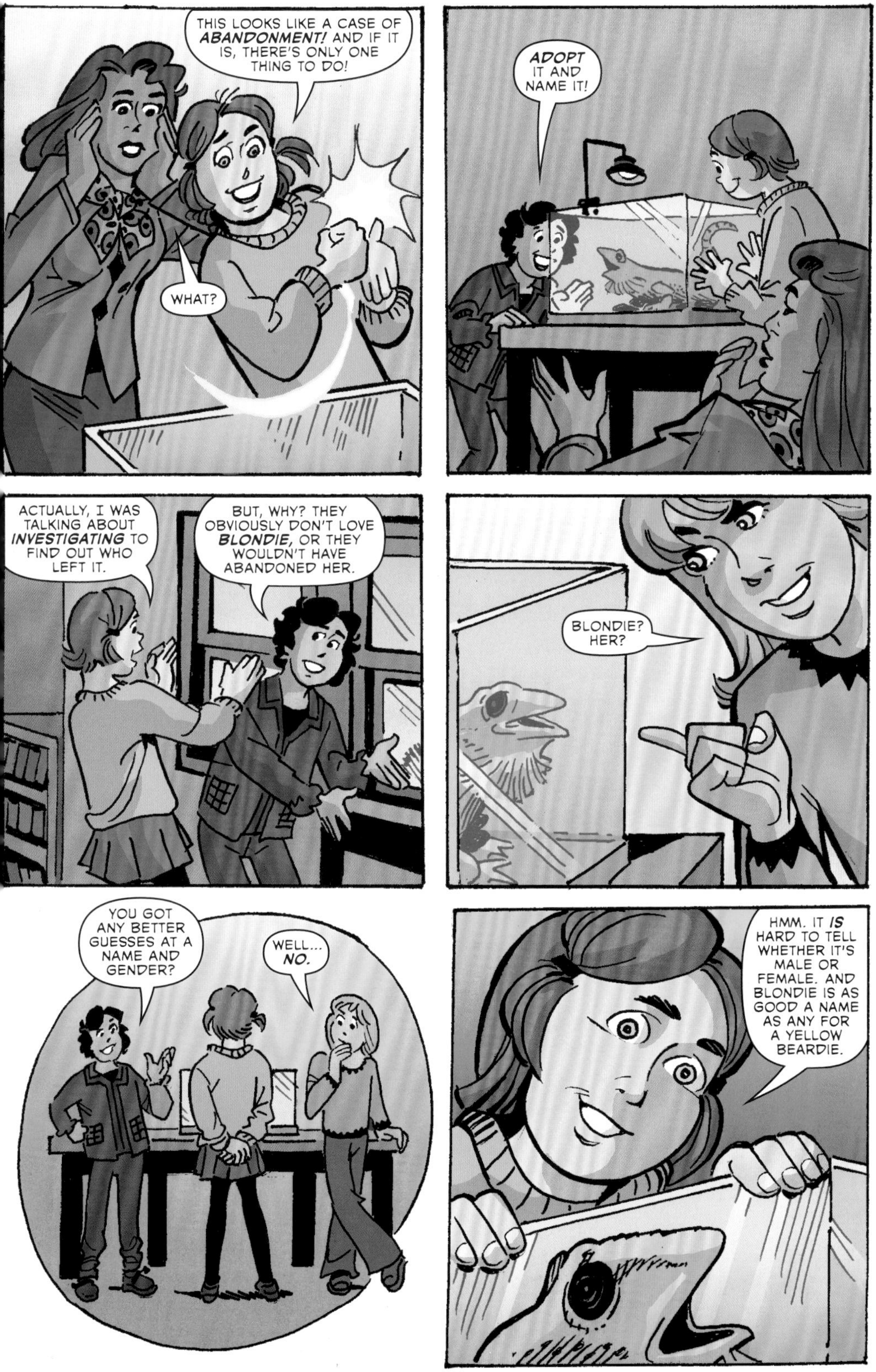
THIS LOOKS LIKE A CASE OF ABANDONMENT! AND IF IT IS, THERE'S ONLY ONE THING TO DO!
WHAT?
ADOPT IT AND NAME IT!
ACTUALLY, I WAS TALKING ABOUT INVESTIGATING TO FIND OUT WHO LEFT IT.
BUT, WHY? THEY OBVIOUSLY DON'T LOVE BLONDIE, OR THEY WOULDN'T HAVE ABANDONED HER.
BLONDIE? HER?
YOU GOT ANY BETTER GUESSES AT A NAME AND GENDER?
WELL... NO.
HMM. IT IS HARD TO TELL WHETHER IT'S MALE OR FEMALE. AND BLONDIE IS AS GOOD A NAME AS ANY FOR A YELLOW BEARDIE.

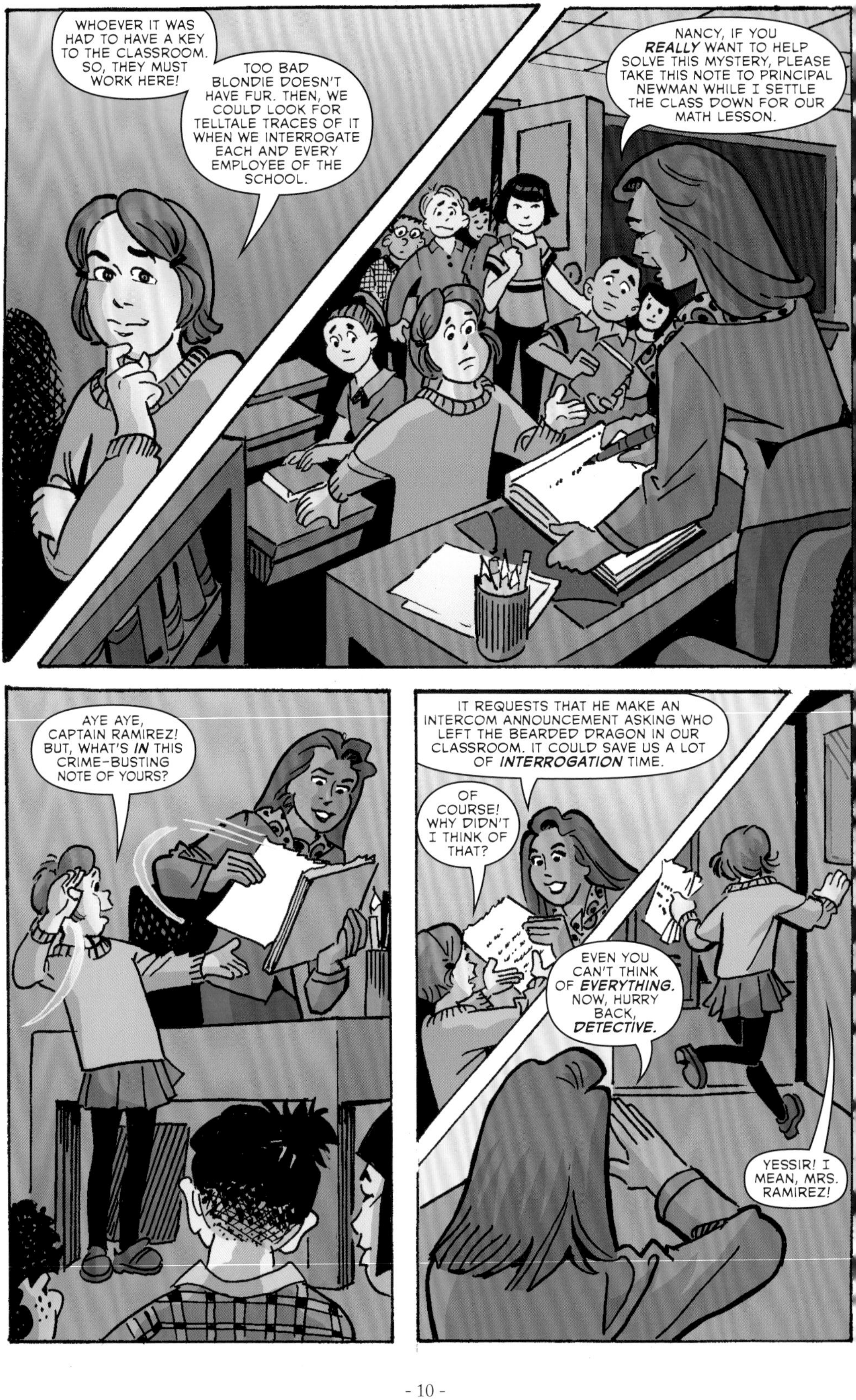
WHOEVER IT WAS HAD TO HAVE A KEY TO THE CLASSROOM. SO, THEY MUST WORK HERE!
TOO BAD BLONDIE DOESN'T HAVE FUR. THEN, WE COULD LOOK FOR TELLTALE TRACES OF IT WHEN WE INTERROGATE EACH AND EVERY EMPLOYEE OF THE SCHOOL.
NANCY, IF YOU REALLY WANT TO HELP SOLVE THIS MYSTERY, PLEASE TAKE THIS NOTE TO PRINCIPAL NEWMAN WHILE I SETTLE THE CLASS DOWN FOR OUR MATH LESSON.
AYE AYE, CAPTAIN RAMIREZ! BUT, WHAT'S IN THIS CRIME-BUSTING NOTE OF YOURS?
IT REQUESTS THAT HE MAKE AN INTERCOM ANNOUNCEMENT ASKING WHO LEFT THE BEARDED DRAGON IN OUR CLASSROOM. IT COULD SAVE US A LOT OF INTERROGATION TIME.
OF COURSE! WHY DIDN'T I THINK OF THAT?
EVEN YOU CAN'T THINK OF EVERYTHING. NOW, HURRY BACK, DETECTIVE.
YESSIR! I MEAN, MRS. RAMIREZ!

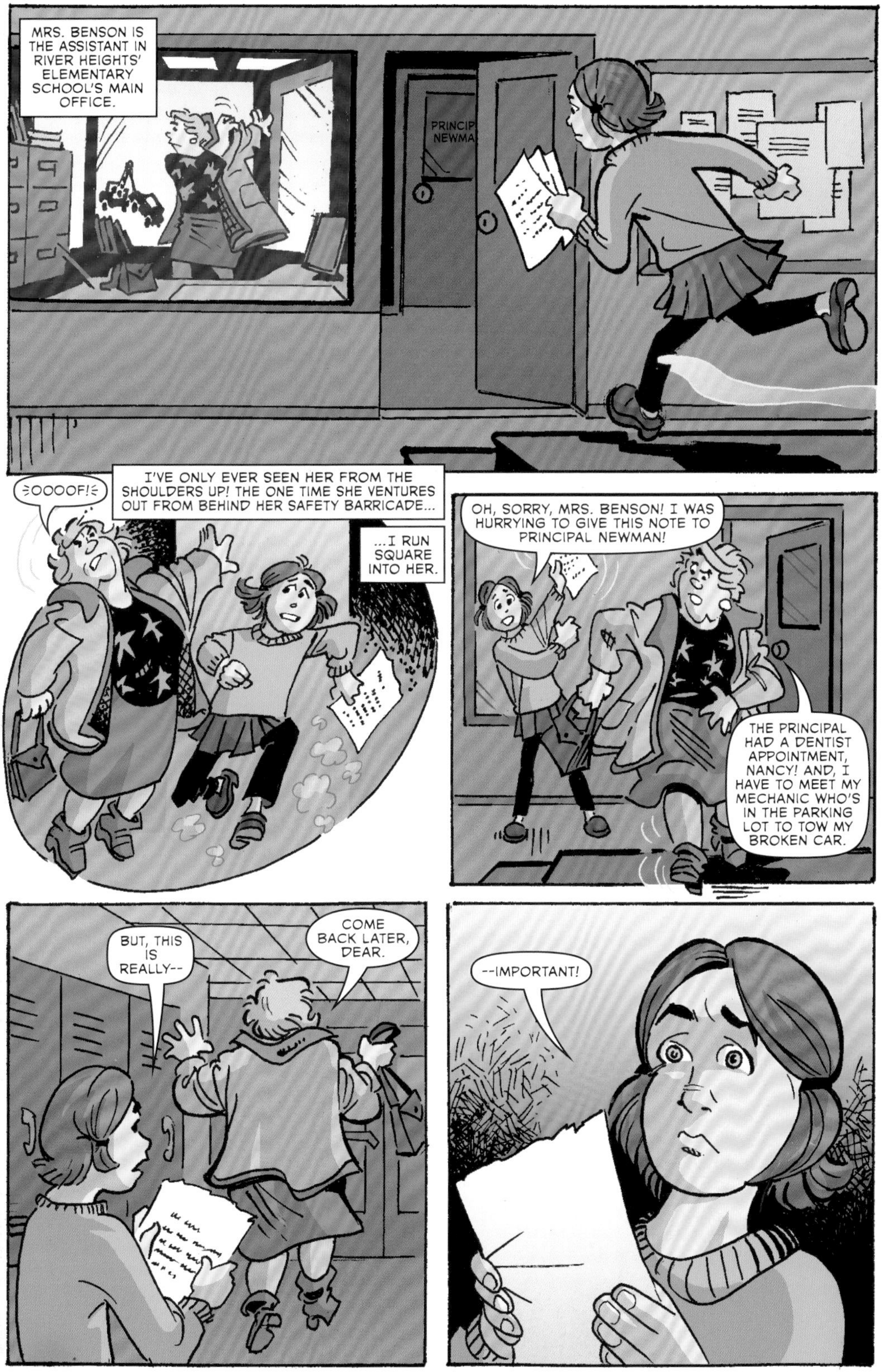
MRS. BENSON IS THE ASSISTANT IN RIVER HEIGHTS' ELEMENTARY SCHOOL'S MAIN OFFICE.
PRINCIP
NEWMA
I'VE ONLY EVER SEEN HER FROM THE SHOULDERS UP! THE ONE TIME SHE VENTURES OUT FROM BEHIND HER SAFETY BARRICADE...
OOOOF!
...I RUN SQUARE INTO HER.
OH, SORRY, MRS. BENSON! I WAS HURRYING TO GIVE THIS NOTE TO PRINCIPAL NEWMAN!
THE PRINCIPAL HAD A DENTIST APPOINTMENT, NANCY! AND, I HAVE TO MEET MY MECHANIC WHO'S IN THE PARKING LOT TO TOW MY BROKEN CAR.
BUT, THIS IS REALLY--
COME BACK LATER, DEAR.
--IMPORTANT!

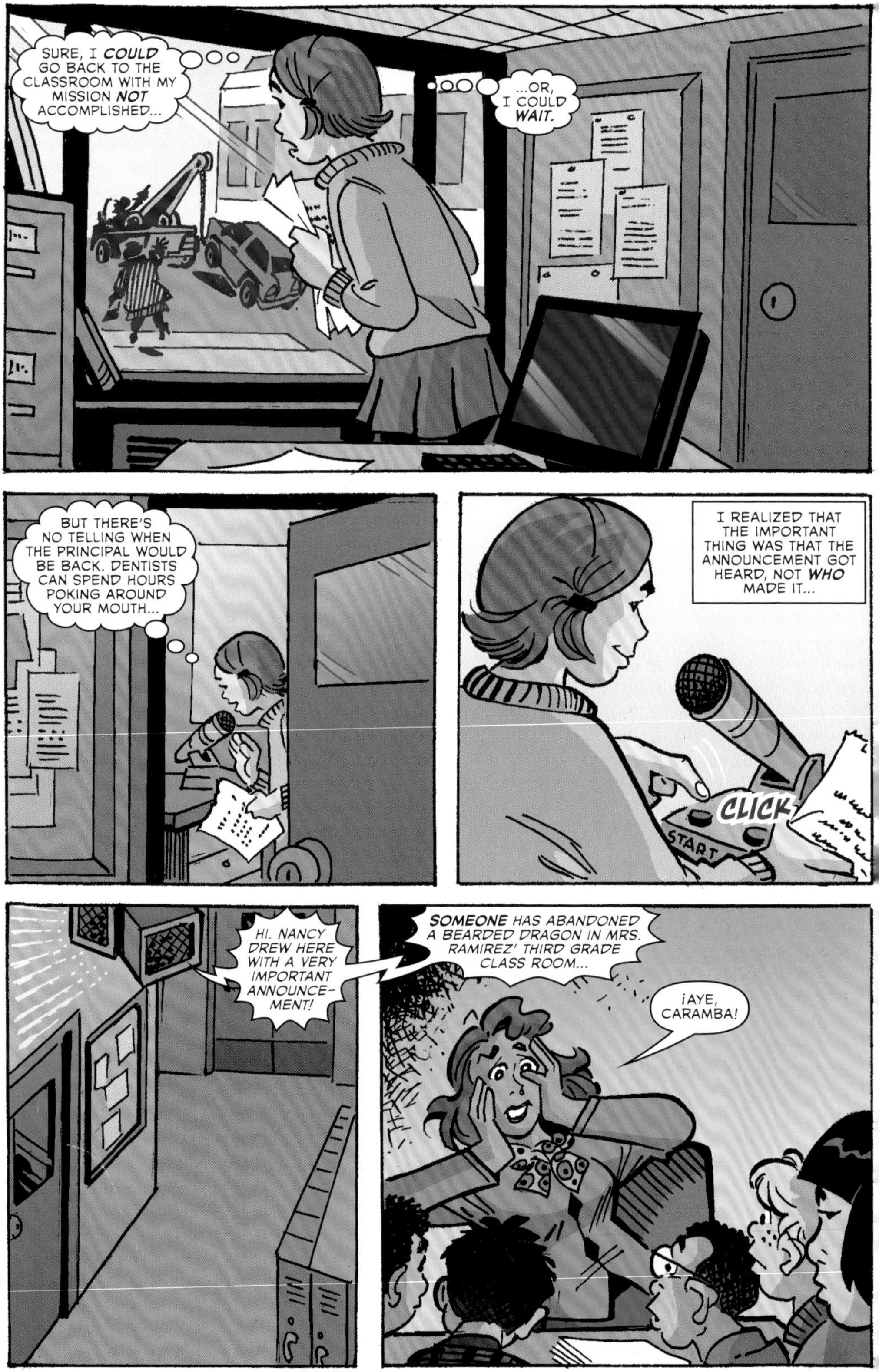
SURE, I *COULD* GO BACK TO THE CLASSROOM WITH MY MISSION *NOT* ACCOMPLISHED...
...OR, I COULD *WAIT.*
BUT THERE'S NO TELLING WHEN THE PRINCIPAL WOULD BE BACK. DENTISTS CAN SPEND HOURS POKING AROUND YOUR MOUTH...
I REALIZED THAT THE IMPORTANT THING WAS THAT THE ANNOUNCEMENT GOT HEARD, NOT *WHO* MADE IT...
START
CLICK
HI. NANCY DREW HERE WITH A VERY IMPORTANT ANNOUNCE-MENT!
SOMEONE HAS ABANDONED A BEARDED DRAGON IN MRS. RAMIREZ' THIRD GRADE CLASS ROOM...
¡AYE, CARAMBA!

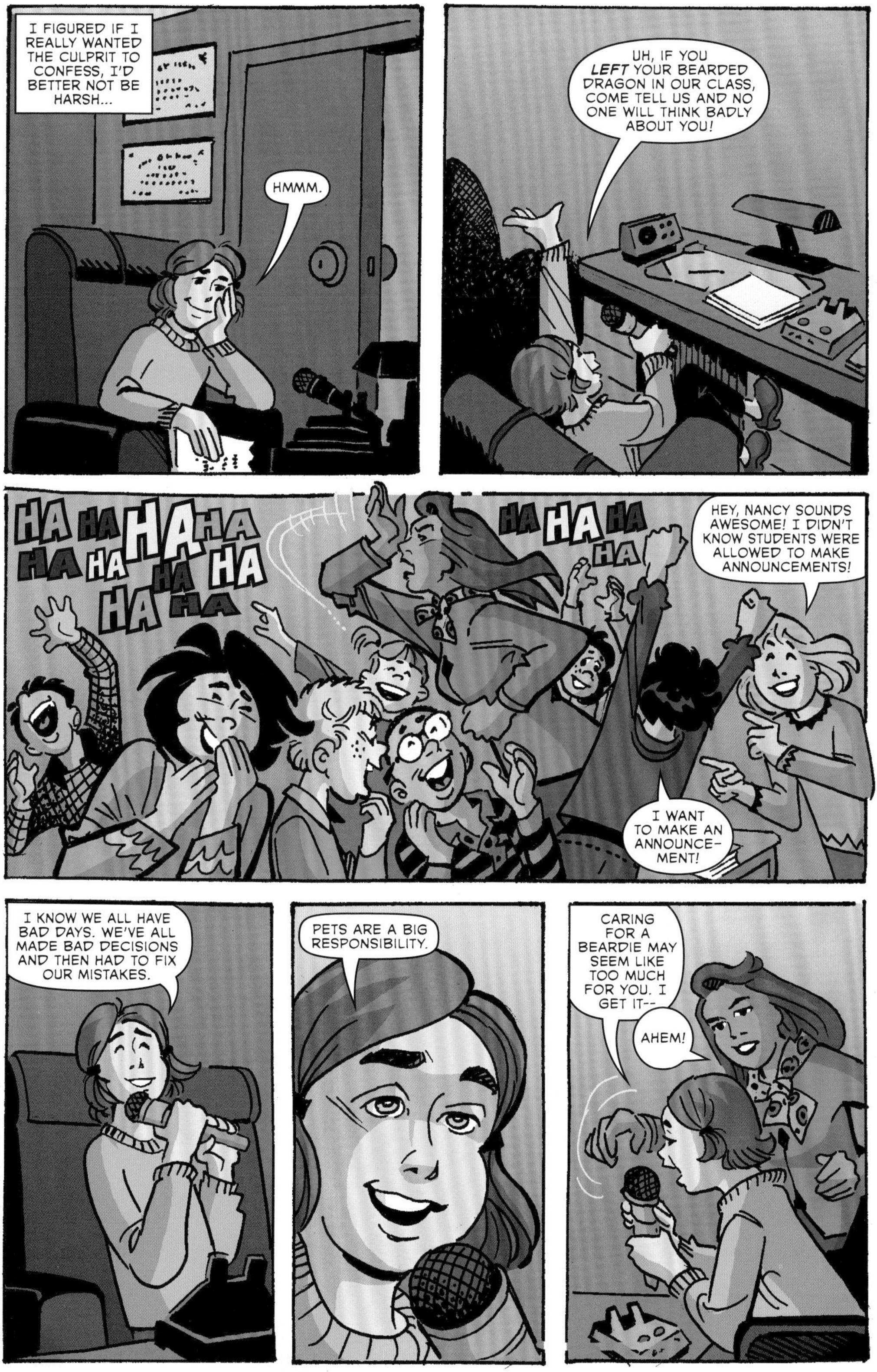
I FIGURED IF I REALLY WANTED THE CULPRIT TO CONFESS, I'D BETTER NOT BE HARSH...
HMMM.
UH, IF YOU LEFT YOUR BEARDED DRAGON IN OUR CLASS, COME TELL US AND NO ONE WILL THINK BADLY ABOUT YOU!
HA HA HA HA HA HA HA HA HA HA HA HA
HA HA HA HA
HEY, NANCY SOUNDS AWESOME! I DIDN'T KNOW STUDENTS WERE ALLOWED TO MAKE ANNOUNCEMENTS!
I WANT TO MAKE AN ANNOUNCE-MENT!
I KNOW WE ALL HAVE BAD DAYS. WE'VE ALL MADE BAD DECISIONS AND THEN HAD TO FIX OUR MISTAKES.
PETS ARE A BIG RESPONSIBILITY.
CARING FOR A BEARDIE MAY SEEM LIKE TOO MUCH FOR YOU. I GET IT--
AHEM!

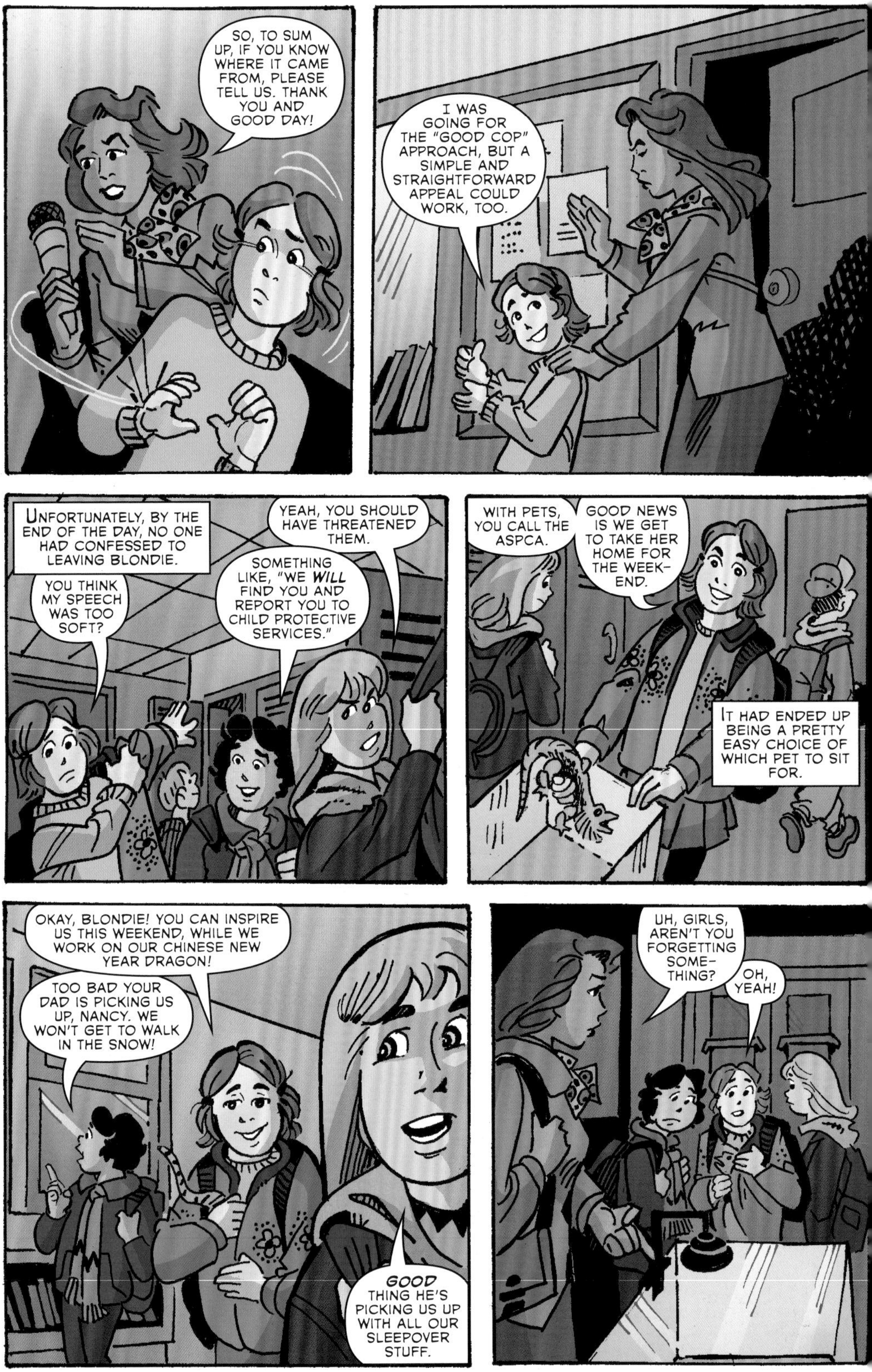
SO, TO SUM UP, IF YOU KNOW WHERE IT CAME FROM, PLEASE TELL US. THANK YOU AND GOOD DAY!
I WAS GOING FOR THE "GOOD COP" APPROACH, BUT A SIMPLE AND STRAIGHTFORWARD APPEAL COULD WORK, TOO.
UNFORTUNATELY, BY THE END OF THE DAY, NO ONE HAD CONFESSED TO LEAVING BLONDIE.
YOU THINK MY SPEECH WAS TOO SOFT?
YEAH, YOU SHOULD HAVE THREATENED THEM.
SOMETHING LIKE, "WE WILL FIND YOU AND REPORT YOU TO CHILD PROTECTIVE SERVICES."
WITH PETS, YOU CALL THE ASPCA.
GOOD NEWS IS WE GET TO TAKE HER HOME FOR THE WEEK-END.
IT HAD ENDED UP BEING A PRETTY EASY CHOICE OF WHICH PET TO SIT FOR.
OKAY, BLONDIE! YOU CAN INSPIRE US THIS WEEKEND, WHILE WE WORK ON OUR CHINESE NEW YEAR DRAGON!
TOO BAD YOUR DAD IS PICKING US UP, NANCY. WE WON'T GET TO WALK IN THE SNOW!
GOOD THING HE'S PICKING US UP WITH ALL OUR SLEEPOVER STUFF.
UH, GIRLS, AREN'T YOU FORGETTING SOME-THING?
OH, YEAH!

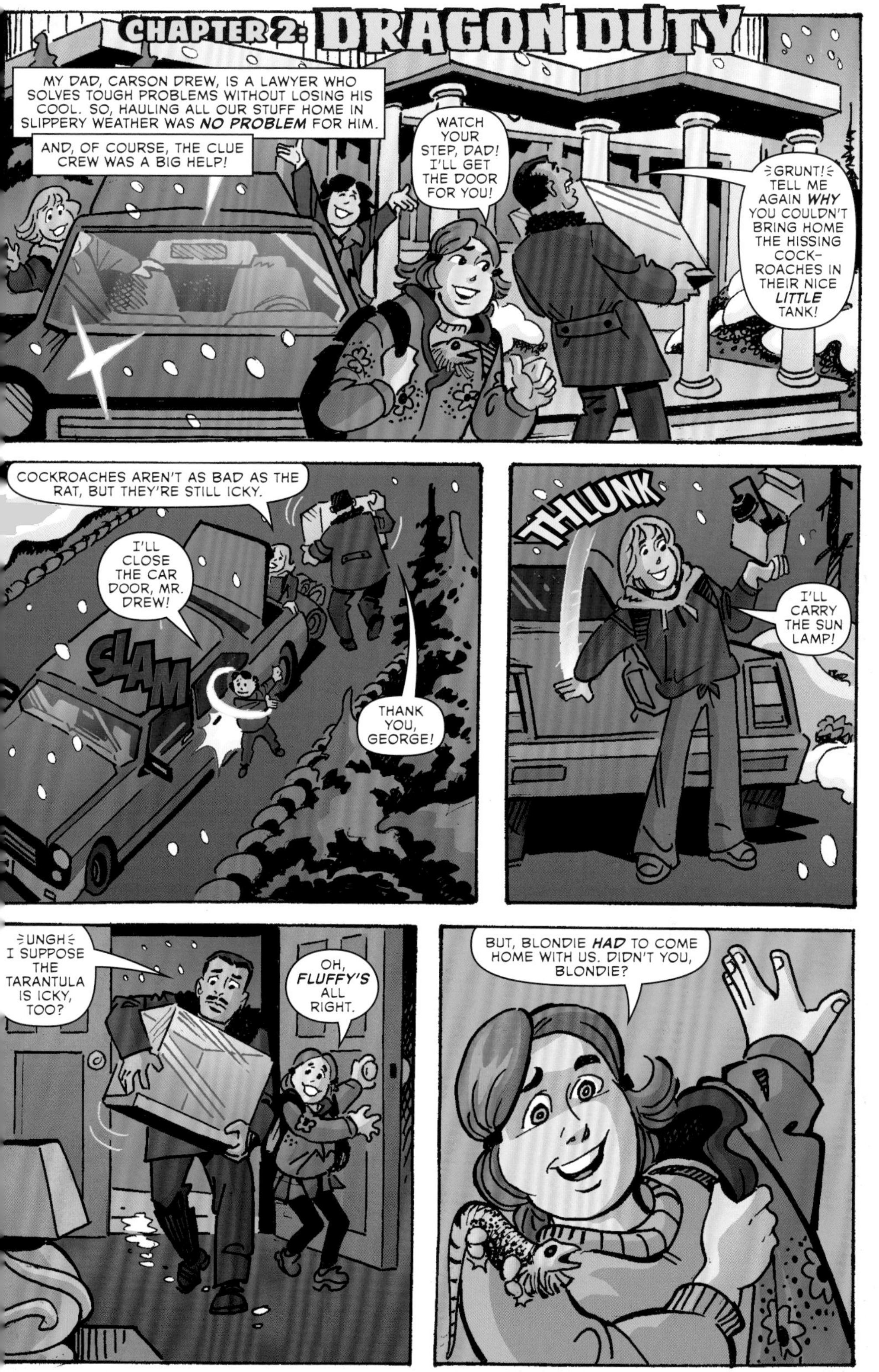
CHAPTER 2: DRAGON DUTY
MY DAD, CARSON DREW, IS A LAWYER WHO SOLVES TOUGH PROBLEMS WITHOUT LOSING HIS COOL. SO, HAULING ALL OUR STUFF HOME IN SLIPPERY WEATHER WAS NO PROBLEM FOR HIM.
AND, OF COURSE, THE CLUE CREW WAS A BIG HELP!
WATCH YOUR STEP, DAD! I'LL GET THE DOOR FOR YOU!
GRUNT! TELL ME AGAIN WHY YOU COULDN'T BRING HOME THE HISSING COCK-ROACHES IN THEIR NICE LITTLE TANK!
COCKROACHES AREN'T AS BAD AS THE RAT, BUT THEY'RE STILL ICKY.
I'LL CLOSE THE CAR DOOR, MR. DREW!
SLAM
THANK YOU, GEORGE!
THLUNK
I'LL CARRY THE SUN LAMP!
UNGH I SUPPOSE THE TARANTULA IS ICKY, TOO?
OH, FLUFFY'S ALL RIGHT.
BUT, BLONDIE HAD TO COME HOME WITH US. DIDN'T YOU, BLONDIE?

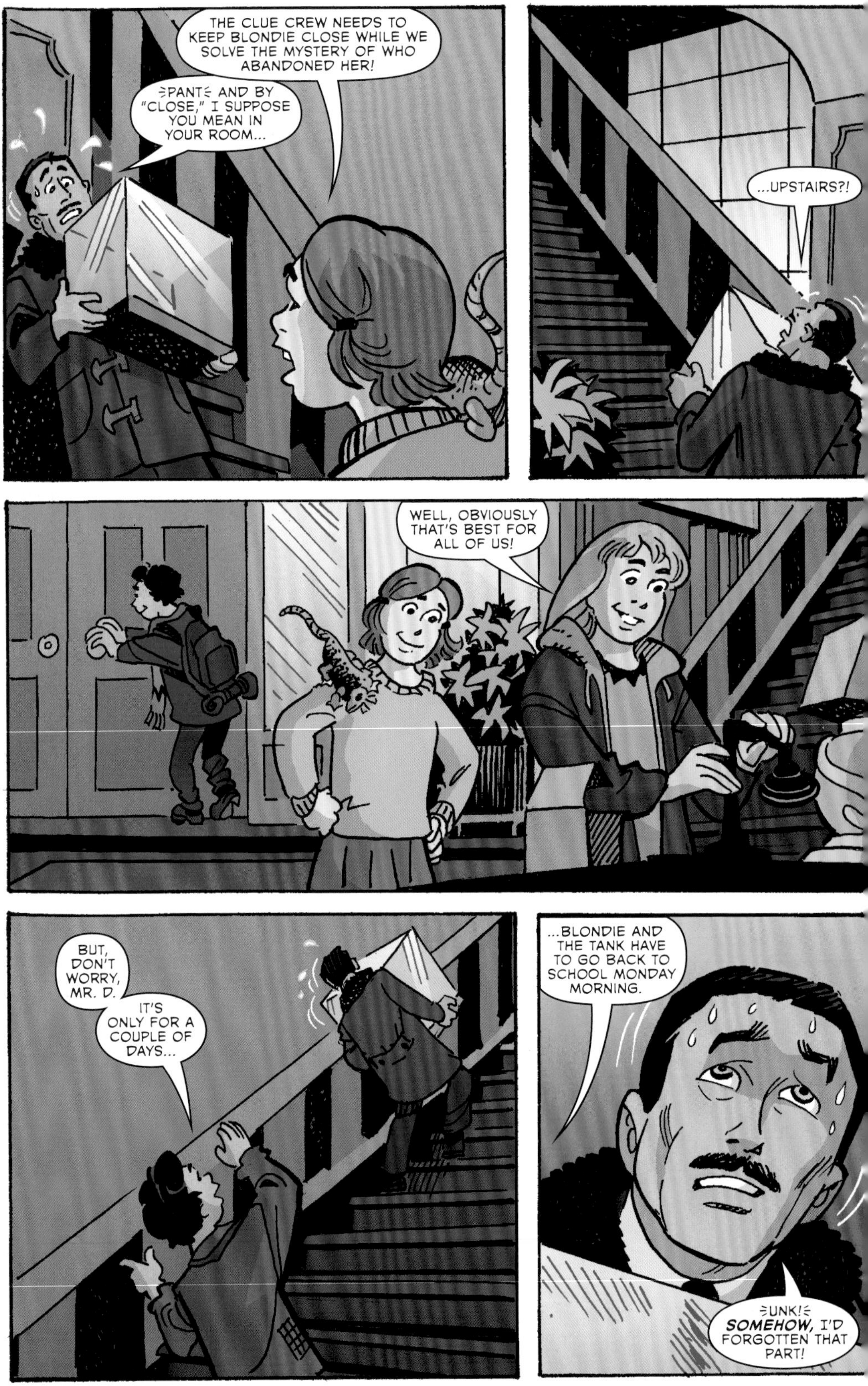
THE CLUE CREW NEEDS TO KEEP BLONDIE CLOSE WHILE WE SOLVE THE MYSTERY OF WHO ABANDONED HER!
⇒PANT⇐ AND BY "CLOSE," I SUPPOSE YOU MEAN IN YOUR ROOM...
...UPSTAIRS?!
WELL, OBVIOUSLY THAT'S BEST FOR ALL OF US!
BUT, DON'T WORRY, MR. D.
IT'S ONLY FOR A COUPLE OF DAYS...
...BLONDIE AND THE TANK HAVE TO GO BACK TO SCHOOL MONDAY MORNING.
⇒UNK!⇐ *SOMEHOW,* I'D FORGOTTEN THAT PART!

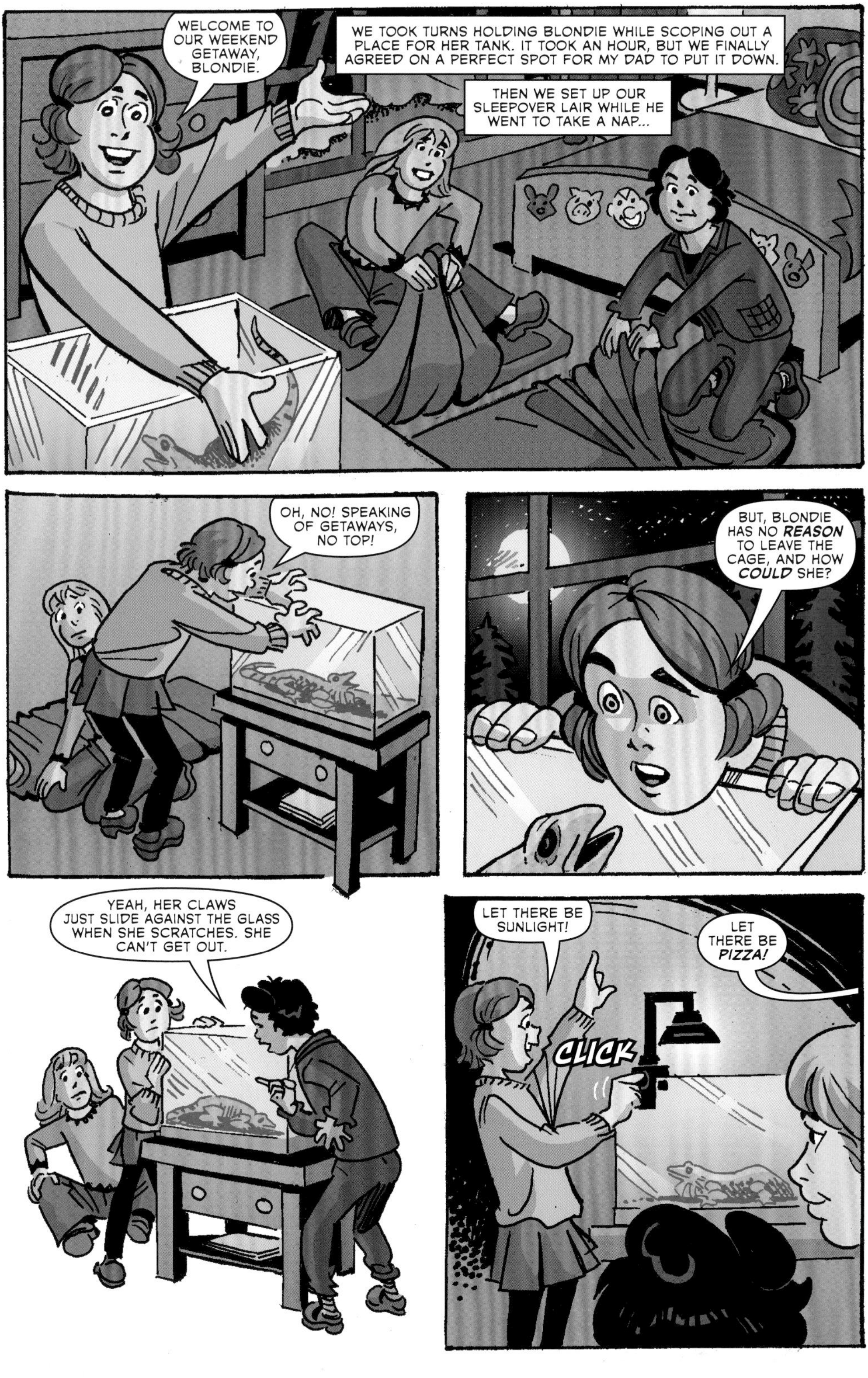
WELCOME TO OUR WEEKEND GETAWAY, BLONDIE.
WE TOOK TURNS HOLDING BLONDIE WHILE SCOPING OUT A PLACE FOR HER TANK. IT TOOK AN HOUR, BUT WE FINALLY AGREED ON A PERFECT SPOT FOR MY DAD TO PUT IT DOWN.
THEN WE SET UP OUR SLEEPOVER LAIR WHILE HE WENT TO TAKE A NAP...
OH, NO! SPEAKING OF GETAWAYS, NO TOP!
BUT, BLONDIE HAS NO REASON TO LEAVE THE CAGE, AND HOW COULD SHE?
YEAH, HER CLAWS JUST SLIDE AGAINST THE GLASS WHEN SHE SCRATCHES. SHE CAN'T GET OUT.
LET THERE BE SUNLIGHT!
LET THERE BE PIZZA!
CLICK

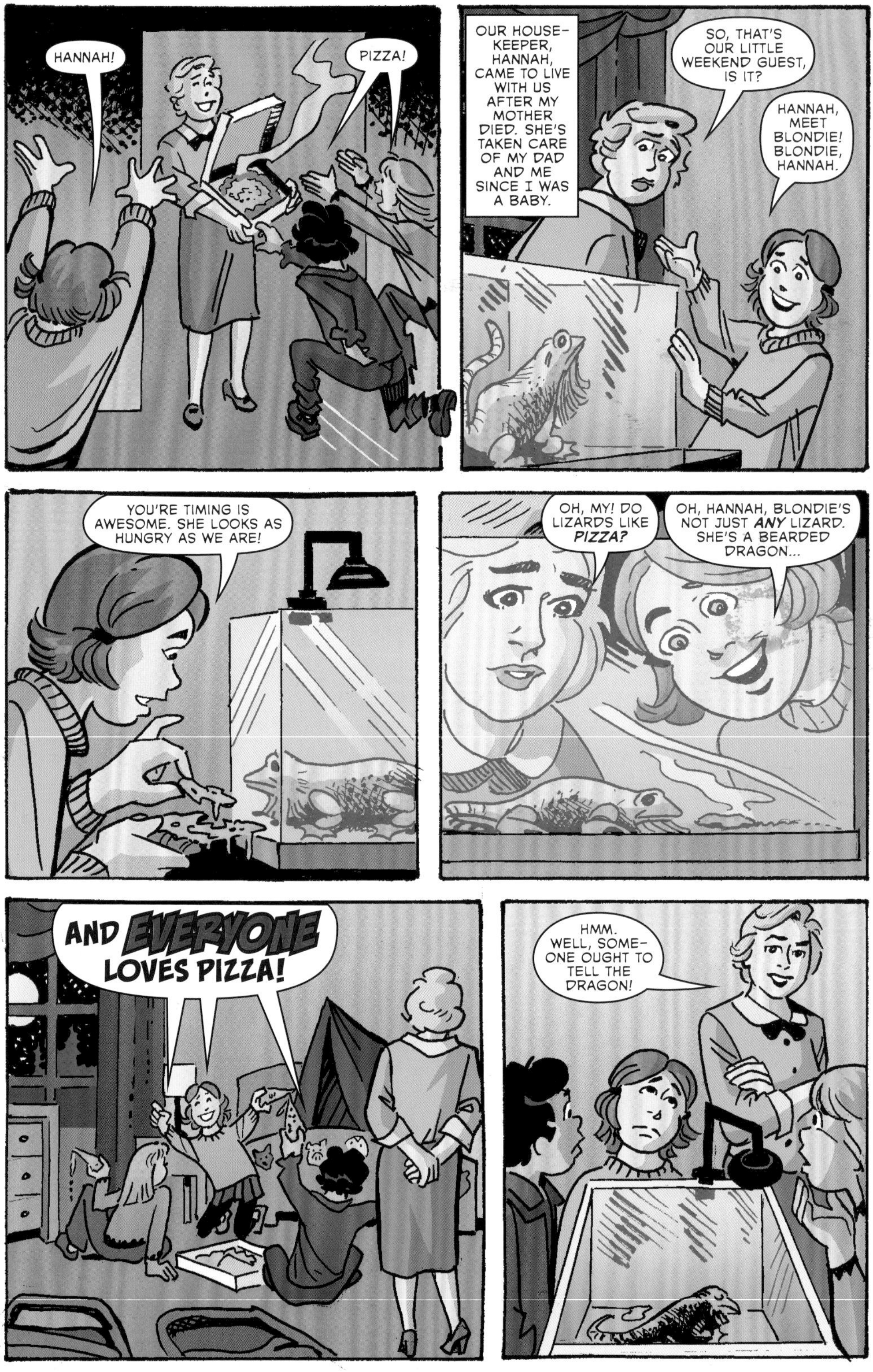
HANNAH!
PIZZA!
OUR HOUSE-KEEPER, HANNAH, CAME TO LIVE WITH US AFTER MY MOTHER DIED. SHE'S TAKEN CARE OF MY DAD AND ME SINCE I WAS A BABY.
SO, THAT'S OUR LITTLE WEEKEND GUEST, IS IT?
HANNAH, MEET BLONDIE! BLONDIE, HANNAH.
YOU'RE TIMING IS AWESOME. SHE LOOKS AS HUNGRY AS WE ARE!
OH, MY! DO LIZARDS LIKE PIZZA?
OH, HANNAH, BLONDIE'S NOT JUST ANY LIZARD. SHE'S A BEARDED DRAGON...
AND EVERYONE LOVES PIZZA!
HMM. WELL, SOME-ONE OUGHT TO TELL THE DRAGON!

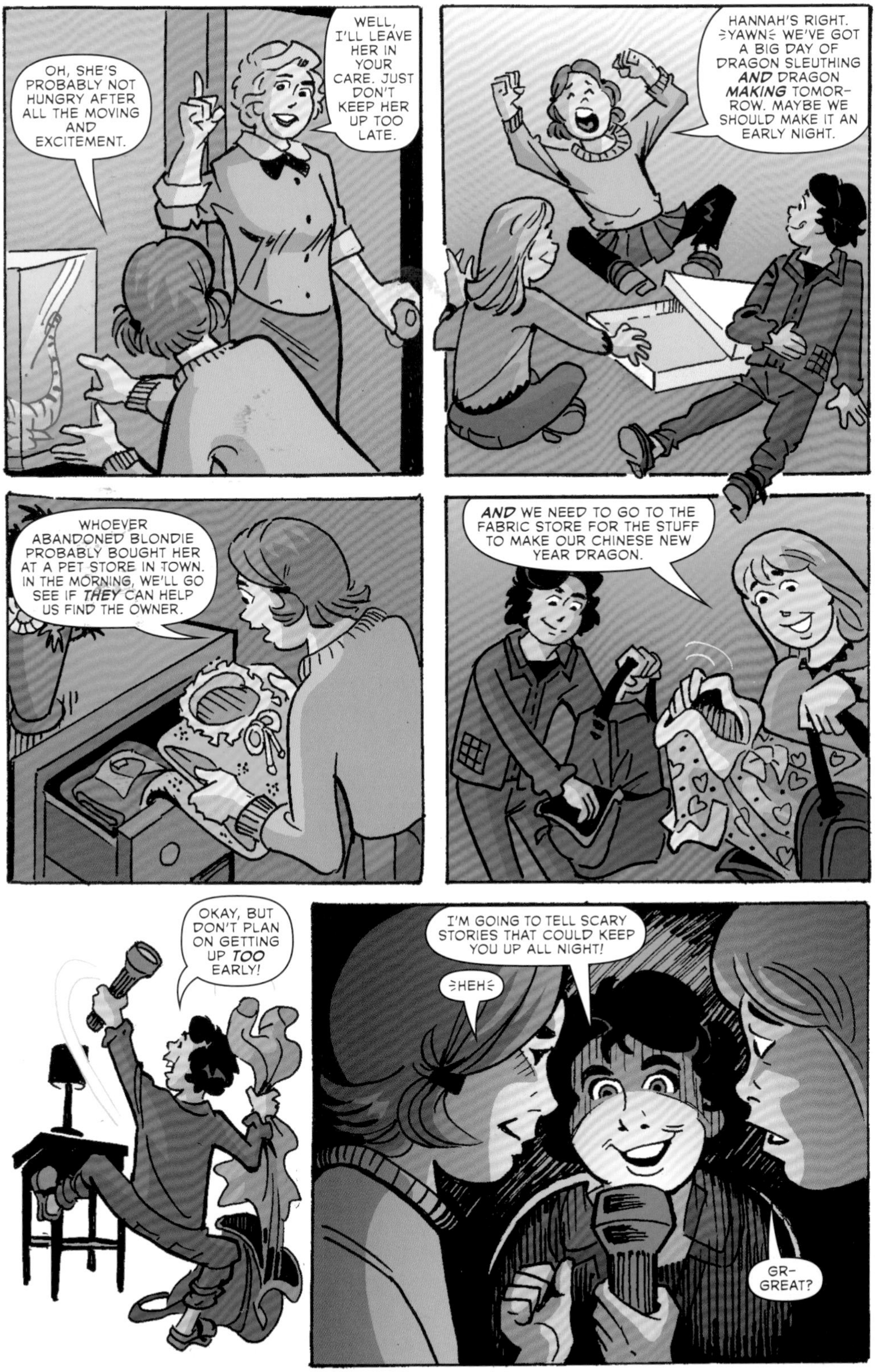
OH, SHE'S PROBABLY NOT HUNGRY AFTER ALL THE MOVING AND EXCITEMENT.
WELL, I'LL LEAVE HER IN YOUR CARE. JUST DON'T KEEP HER UP TOO LATE.
HANNAH'S RIGHT. ⋛YAWN⋚ WE'VE GOT A BIG DAY OF DRAGON SLEUTHING *AND* DRAGON *MAKING* TOMORROW. MAYBE WE SHOULD MAKE IT AN EARLY NIGHT.
WHOEVER ABANDONED BLONDIE PROBABLY BOUGHT HER AT A PET STORE IN TOWN. IN THE MORNING, WE'LL GO SEE IF *THEY* CAN HELP US FIND THE OWNER.
AND WE NEED TO GO TO THE FABRIC STORE FOR THE STUFF TO MAKE OUR CHINESE NEW YEAR DRAGON.
OKAY, BUT DON'T PLAN ON GETTING UP *TOO* EARLY!
I'M GOING TO TELL SCARY STORIES THAT COULD KEEP YOU UP ALL NIGHT!
⋛HEH⋚
GR-GREAT?

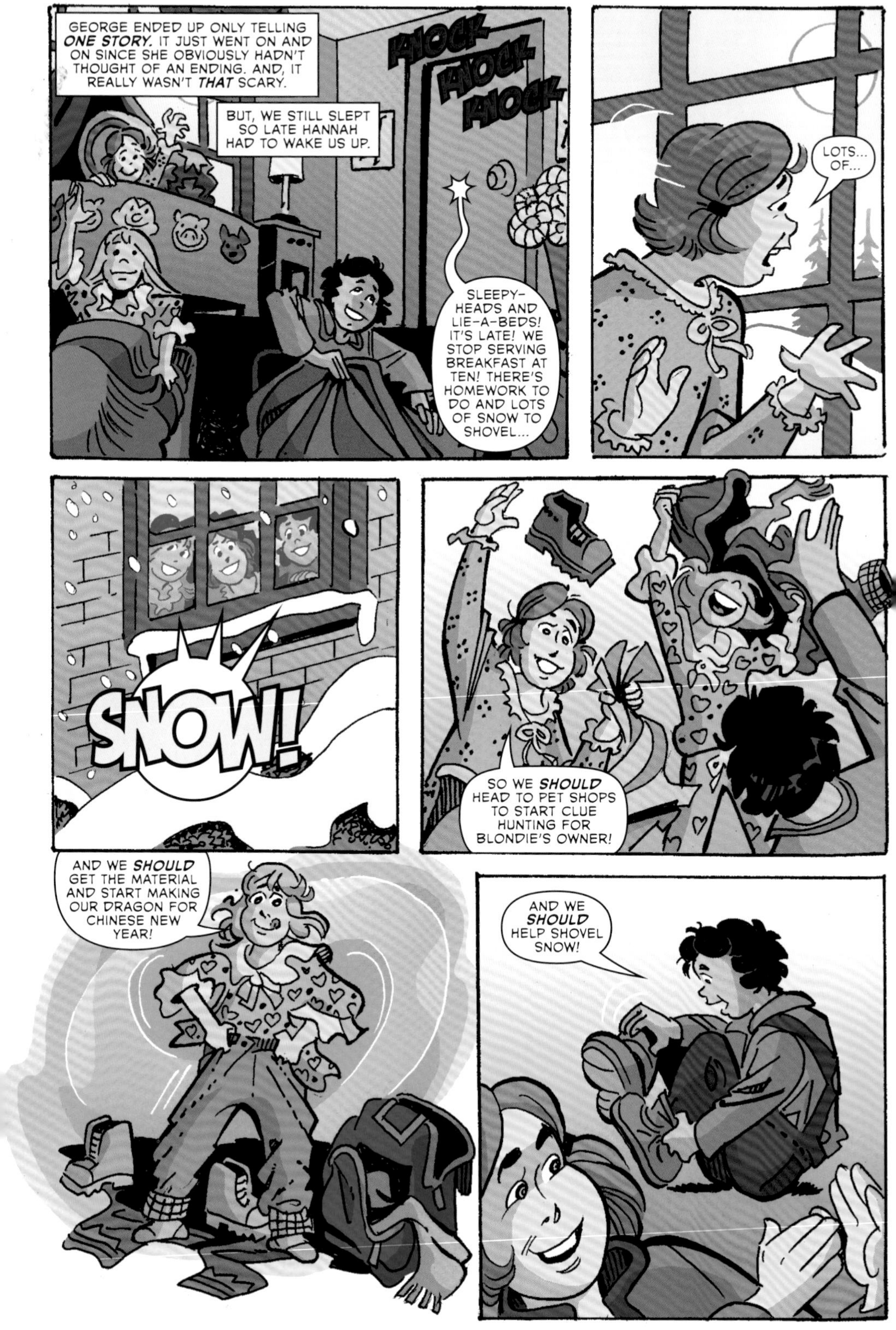
GEORGE ENDED UP ONLY TELLING ONE STORY. IT JUST WENT ON AND ON SINCE SHE OBVIOUSLY HADN'T THOUGHT OF AN ENDING. AND, IT REALLY WASN'T THAT SCARY.
KNOCK KNOCK KNOCK
BUT, WE STILL SLEPT SO LATE HANNAH HAD TO WAKE US UP.
SLEEPY-HEADS AND LIE-A-BEDS! IT'S LATE! WE STOP SERVING BREAKFAST AT TEN! THERE'S HOMEWORK TO DO AND LOTS OF SNOW TO SHOVEL...
LOTS... OF...
SNOW!
SO WE SHOULD HEAD TO PET SHOPS TO START CLUE HUNTING FOR BLONDIE'S OWNER!
AND WE SHOULD GET THE MATERIAL AND START MAKING OUR DRAGON FOR CHINESE NEW YEAR!
AND WE SHOULD HELP SHOVEL SNOW!

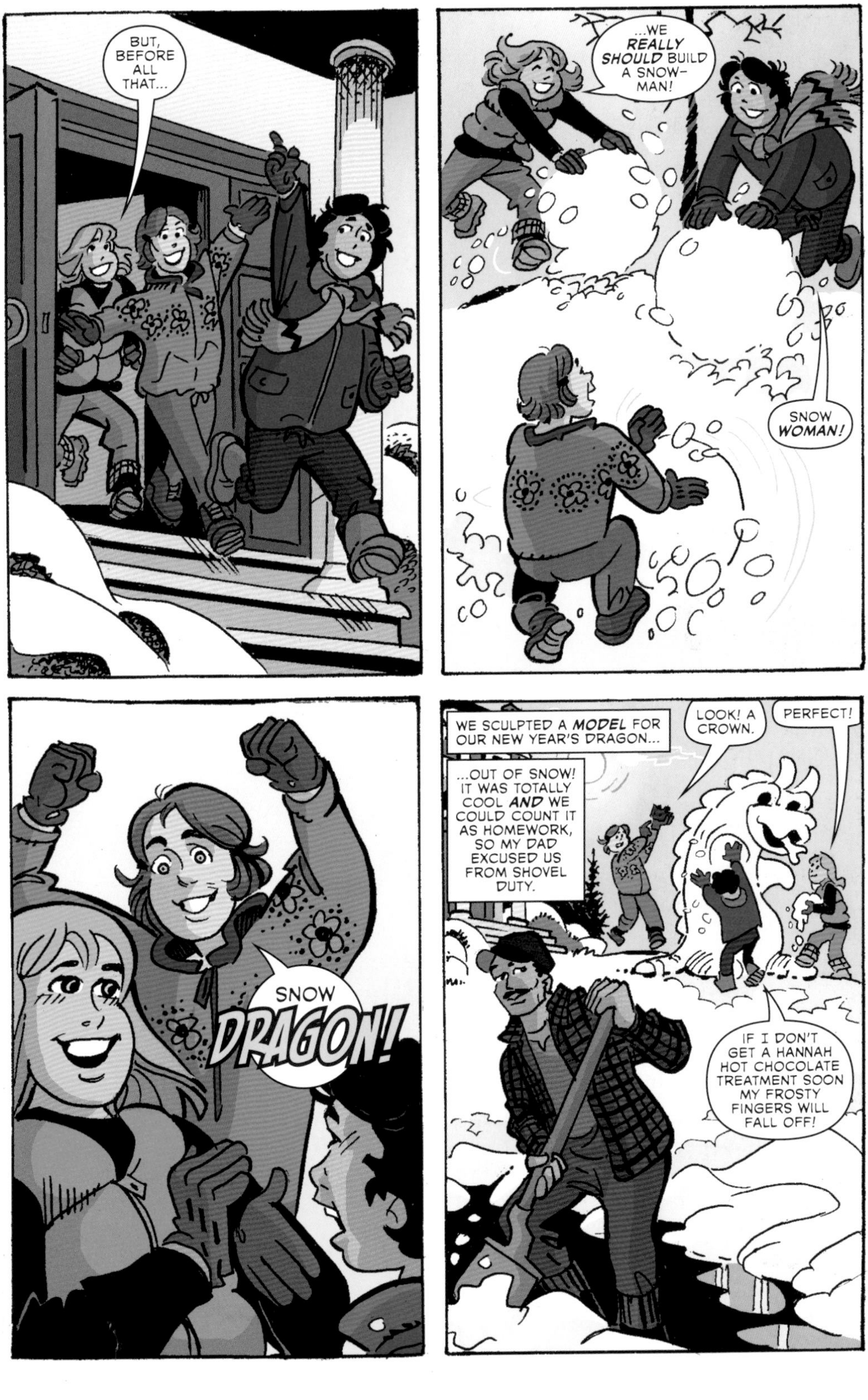
BUT, BEFORE ALL THAT...
...WE REALLY SHOULD BUILD A SNOW-MAN!
SNOW WOMAN!
SNOW DRAGON!
WE SCULPTED A MODEL FOR OUR NEW YEAR'S DRAGON...
...OUT OF SNOW! IT WAS TOTALLY COOL AND WE COULD COUNT IT AS HOMEWORK, SO MY DAD EXCUSED US FROM SHOVEL DUTY.
LOOK! A CROWN.
PERFECT!
IF I DON'T GET A HANNAH HOT CHOCOLATE TREATMENT SOON MY FROSTY FINGERS WILL FALL OFF!

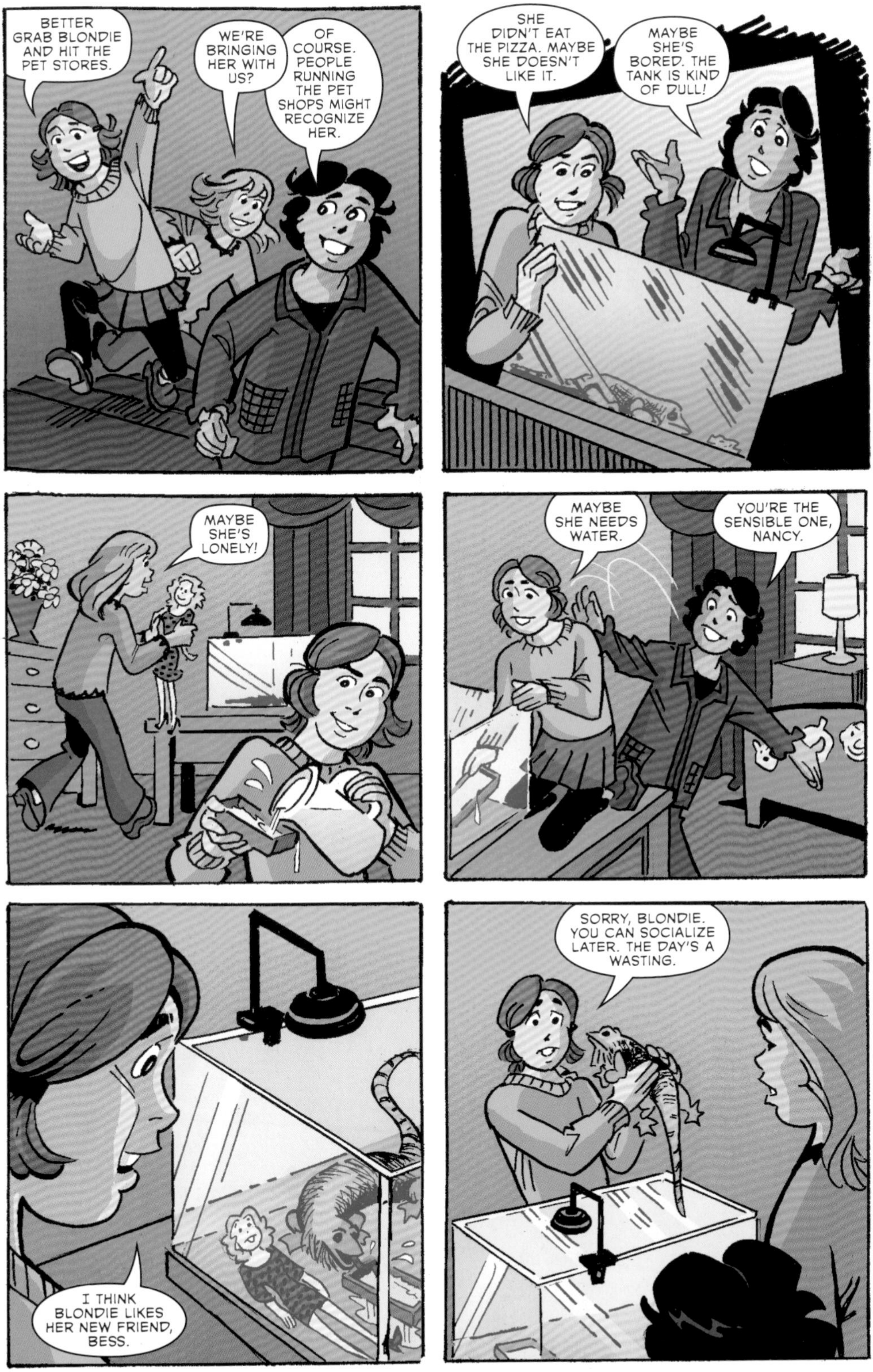
BETTER GRAB BLONDIE AND HIT THE PET STORES.
WE'RE BRINGING HER WITH US?
OF COURSE. PEOPLE RUNNING THE PET SHOPS MIGHT RECOGNIZE HER.
SHE DIDN'T EAT THE PIZZA. MAYBE SHE DOESN'T LIKE IT.
MAYBE SHE'S BORED. THE TANK IS KIND OF DULL!
MAYBE SHE'S LONELY!
MAYBE SHE NEEDS WATER.
YOU'RE THE SENSIBLE ONE, NANCY.
I THINK BLONDIE LIKES HER NEW FRIEND, BESS.
SORRY, BLONDIE. YOU CAN SOCIALIZE LATER. THE DAY'S A WASTING.

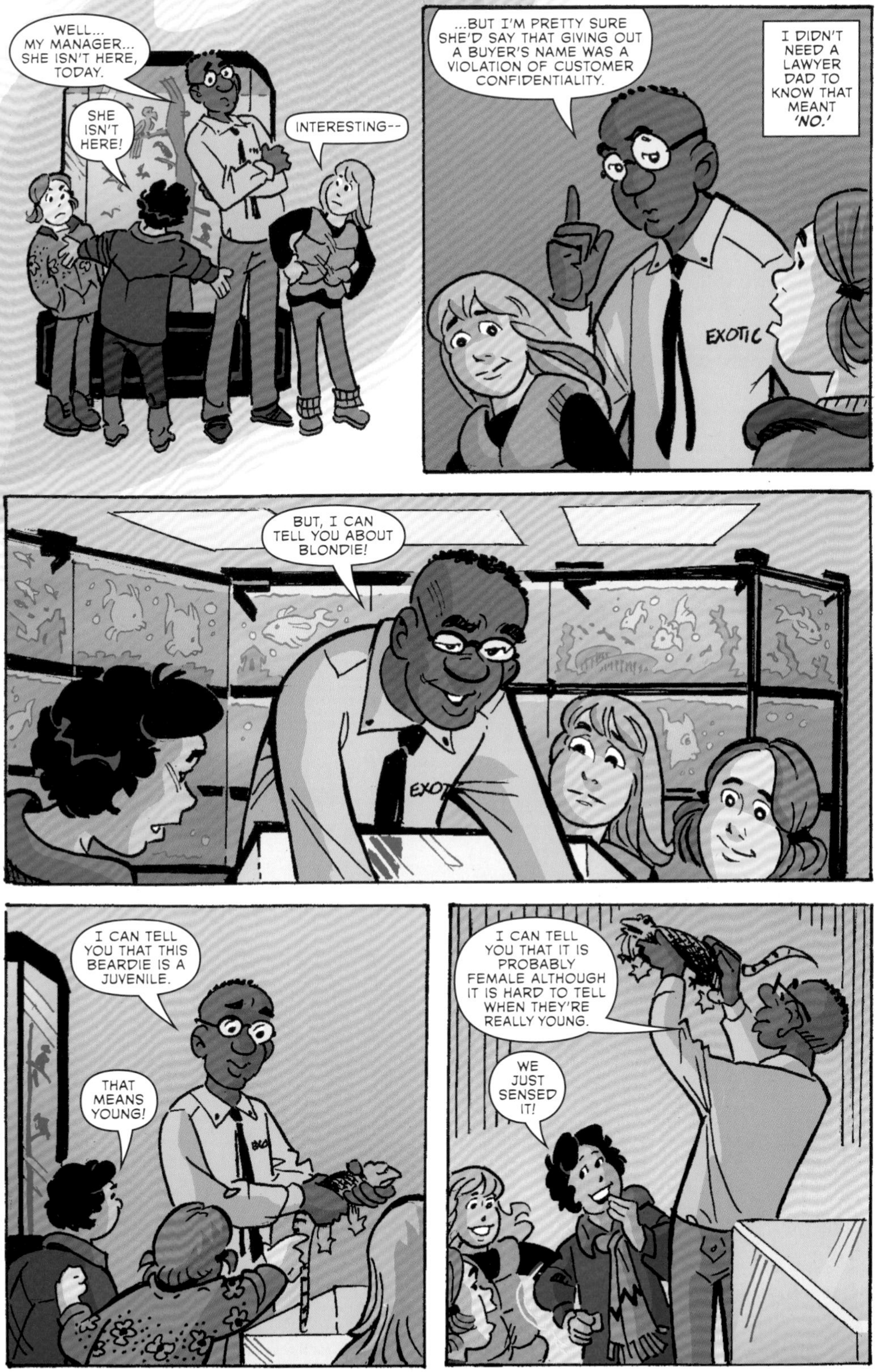

WELL... MY MANAGER... SHE ISN'T HERE, TODAY.
SHE ISN'T HERE!
INTERESTING--
...BUT I'M PRETTY SURE SHE'D SAY THAT GIVING OUT A BUYER'S NAME WAS A VIOLATION OF CUSTOMER CONFIDENTIALITY.
I DIDN'T NEED A LAWYER DAD TO KNOW THAT MEANT *'NO.'*
EXOTIC
BUT, I CAN TELL YOU ABOUT BLONDIE!
I CAN TELL YOU THAT THIS BEARDIE IS A JUVENILE.
THAT MEANS YOUNG!
I CAN TELL YOU THAT IT IS PROBABLY FEMALE ALTHOUGH IT IS HARD TO TELL WHEN THEY'RE REALLY YOUNG.
WE JUST SENSED IT!

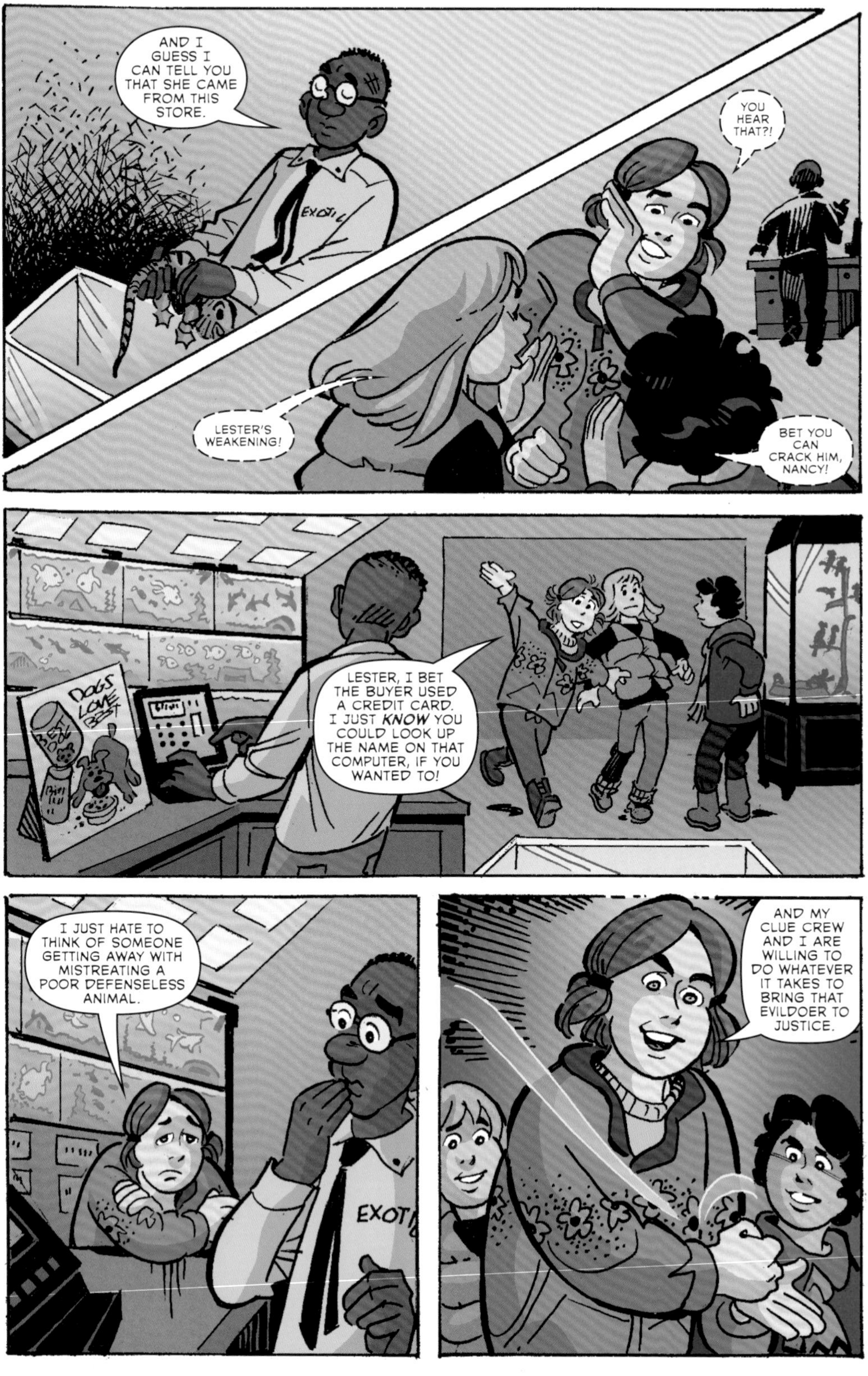
AND I GUESS I CAN TELL YOU THAT SHE CAME FROM THIS STORE.
YOU HEAR THAT?!
LESTER'S WEAKENING!
BET YOU CAN CRACK HIM, NANCY!
DOGS LOVE BEST
LESTER, I BET THE BUYER USED A CREDIT CARD. I JUST KNOW YOU COULD LOOK UP THE NAME ON THAT COMPUTER, IF YOU WANTED TO!
I JUST HATE TO THINK OF SOMEONE GETTING AWAY WITH MISTREATING A POOR DEFENSELESS ANIMAL.
EXOTI
AND MY CLUE CREW AND I ARE WILLING TO DO WHATEVER IT TAKES TO BRING THAT EVILDOER TO JUSTICE.

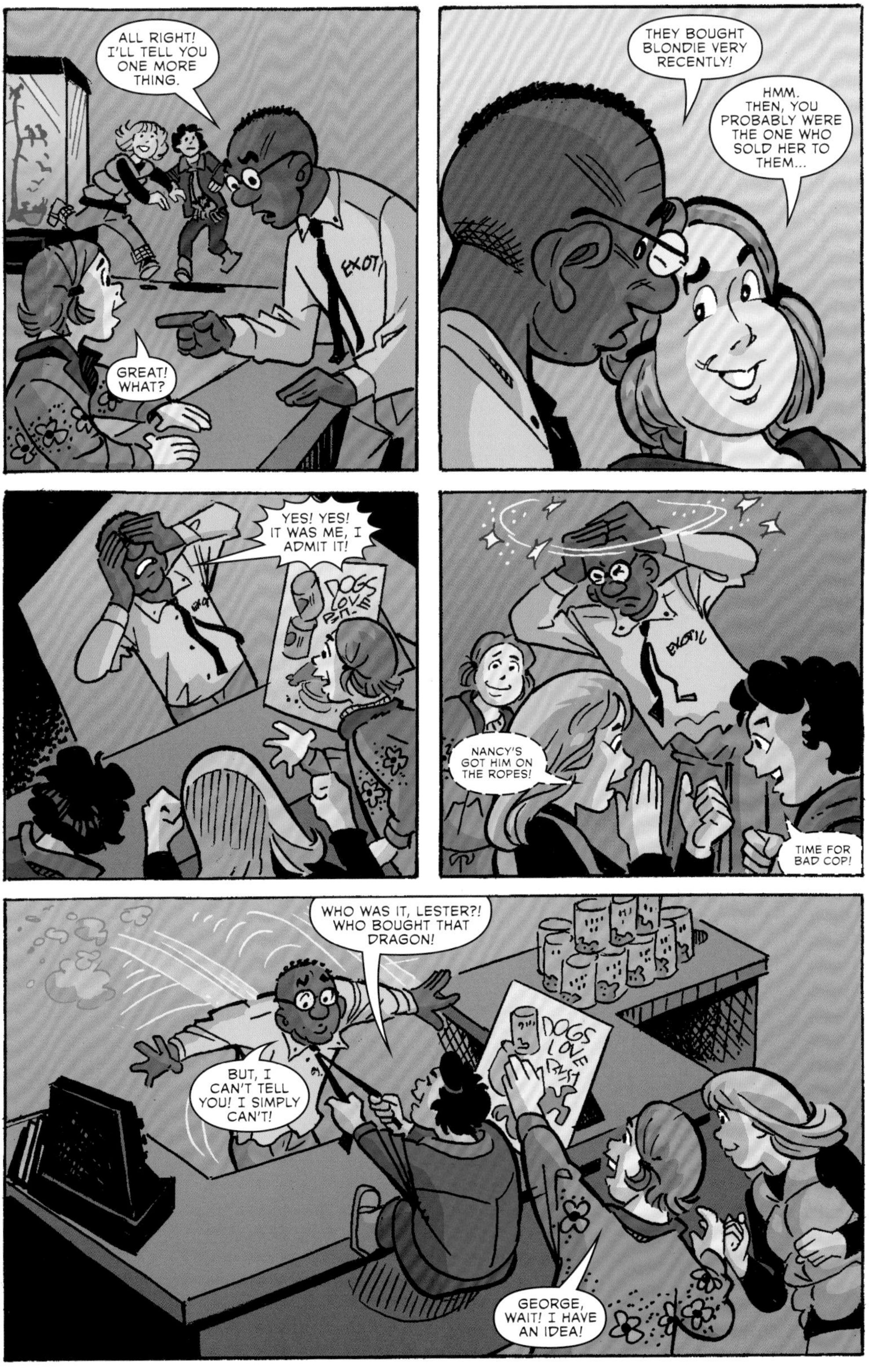
ALL RIGHT! I'LL TELL YOU ONE MORE THING.
GREAT! WHAT?
EXOTI
THEY BOUGHT BLONDIE VERY RECENTLY!
HMM. THEN, YOU PROBABLY WERE THE ONE WHO SOLD HER TO THEM...
YES! YES! IT WAS ME, I ADMIT IT!
DOGS LOVE
NANCY'S GOT HIM ON THE ROPES!
TIME FOR BAD COP!
EXOTIC
WHO WAS IT, LESTER?! WHO BOUGHT THAT DRAGON!
BUT, I CAN'T TELL YOU! I SIMPLY CAN'T!
DOGS LOVE
GEORGE, WAIT! I HAVE AN IDEA!

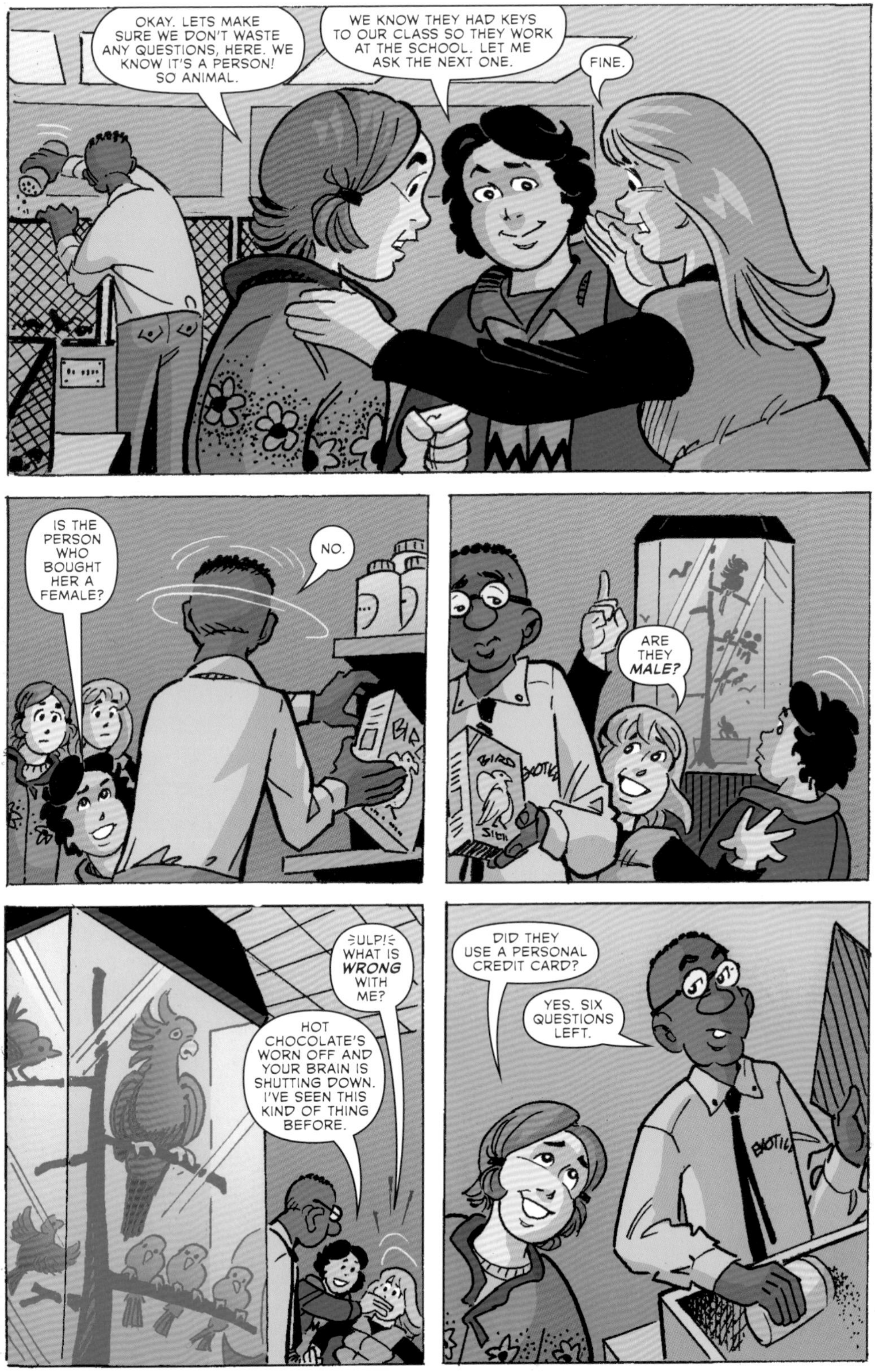
OKAY. LETS MAKE SURE WE DON'T WASTE ANY QUESTIONS, HERE. WE KNOW IT'S A PERSON! SO ANIMAL.
WE KNOW THEY HAD KEYS TO OUR CLASS SO THEY WORK AT THE SCHOOL. LET ME ASK THE NEXT ONE.
FINE.
IS THE PERSON WHO BOUGHT HER A FEMALE?
NO.
ARE THEY MALE?
ULP! WHAT IS WRONG WITH ME?
HOT CHOCOLATE'S WORN OFF AND YOUR BRAIN IS SHUTTING DOWN. I'VE SEEN THIS KIND OF THING BEFORE.
DID THEY USE A PERSONAL CREDIT CARD?
YES. SIX QUESTIONS LEFT.

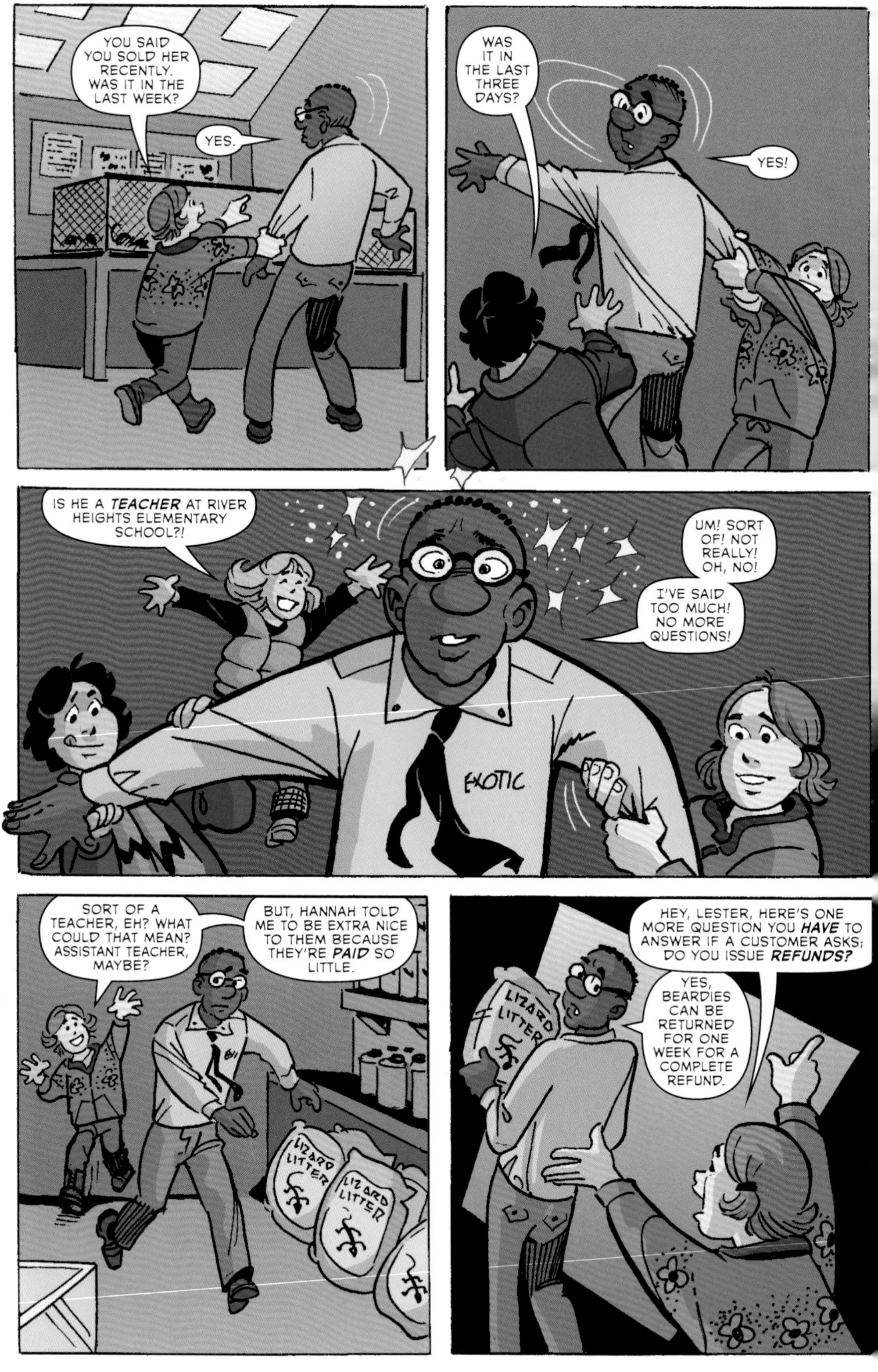

YOU SAID YOU SOLD HER RECENTLY. WAS IT IN THE LAST WEEK?
YES.
WAS IT IN THE LAST THREE DAYS?
YES!
IS HE A ***TEACHER*** AT RIVER HEIGHTS ELEMENTARY SCHOOL?!
UM! SORT OF! NOT REALLY! OH, NO!
I'VE SAID TOO MUCH! NO MORE QUESTIONS!
EXOTIC
SORT OF A TEACHER, EH? WHAT COULD THAT MEAN? ASSISTANT TEACHER, MAYBE?
BUT, HANNAH TOLD ME TO BE EXTRA NICE TO THEM BECAUSE THEY'RE ***PAID*** SO LITTLE.
LIZARD LITTER
LIZARD LITTER
HEY, LESTER, HERE'S ONE MORE QUESTION YOU ***HAVE*** TO ANSWER IF A CUSTOMER ASKS; DO YOU ISSUE ***REFUNDS?***
YES, BEARDIES CAN BE RETURNED FOR ONE WEEK FOR A COMPLETE REFUND.
LIZARD LITTER

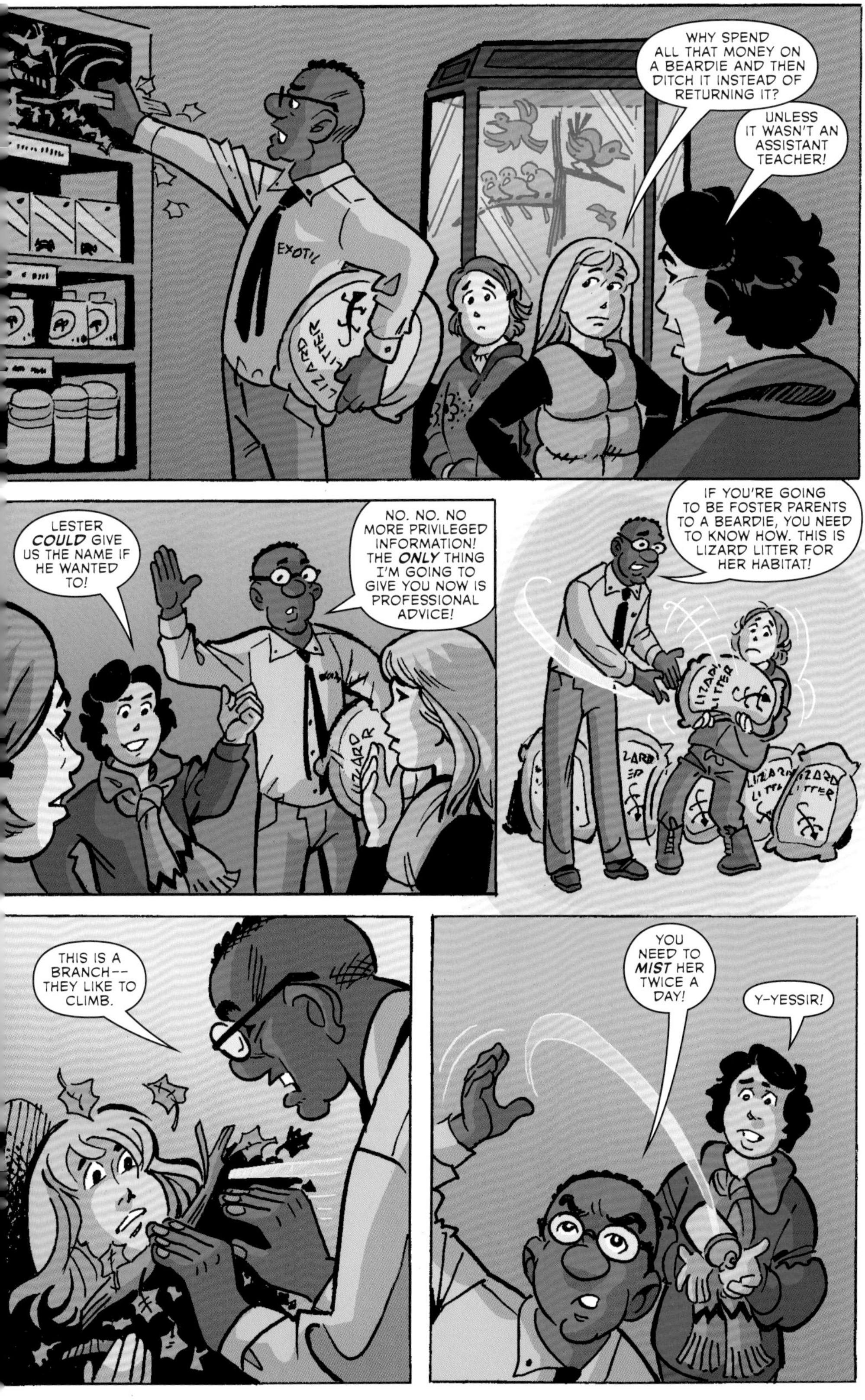
WHY SPEND ALL THAT MONEY ON A BEARDIE AND THEN DITCH IT INSTEAD OF RETURNING IT?
UNLESS IT WASN'T AN ASSISTANT TEACHER!
EXOTIC
LIZARD LITTER
LESTER *COULD* GIVE US THE NAME IF HE WANTED TO!
NO. NO. NO MORE PRIVILEGED INFORMATION! THE *ONLY* THING I'M GOING TO GIVE YOU NOW IS PROFESSIONAL ADVICE!
LIZARD
IF YOU'RE GOING TO BE FOSTER PARENTS TO A BEARDIE, YOU NEED TO KNOW HOW. THIS IS LIZARD LITTER FOR HER HABITAT!
LIZARD LITTER
THIS IS A BRANCH-- THEY LIKE TO CLIMB.
YOU NEED TO *MIST* HER TWICE A DAY!
Y-YESSIR!

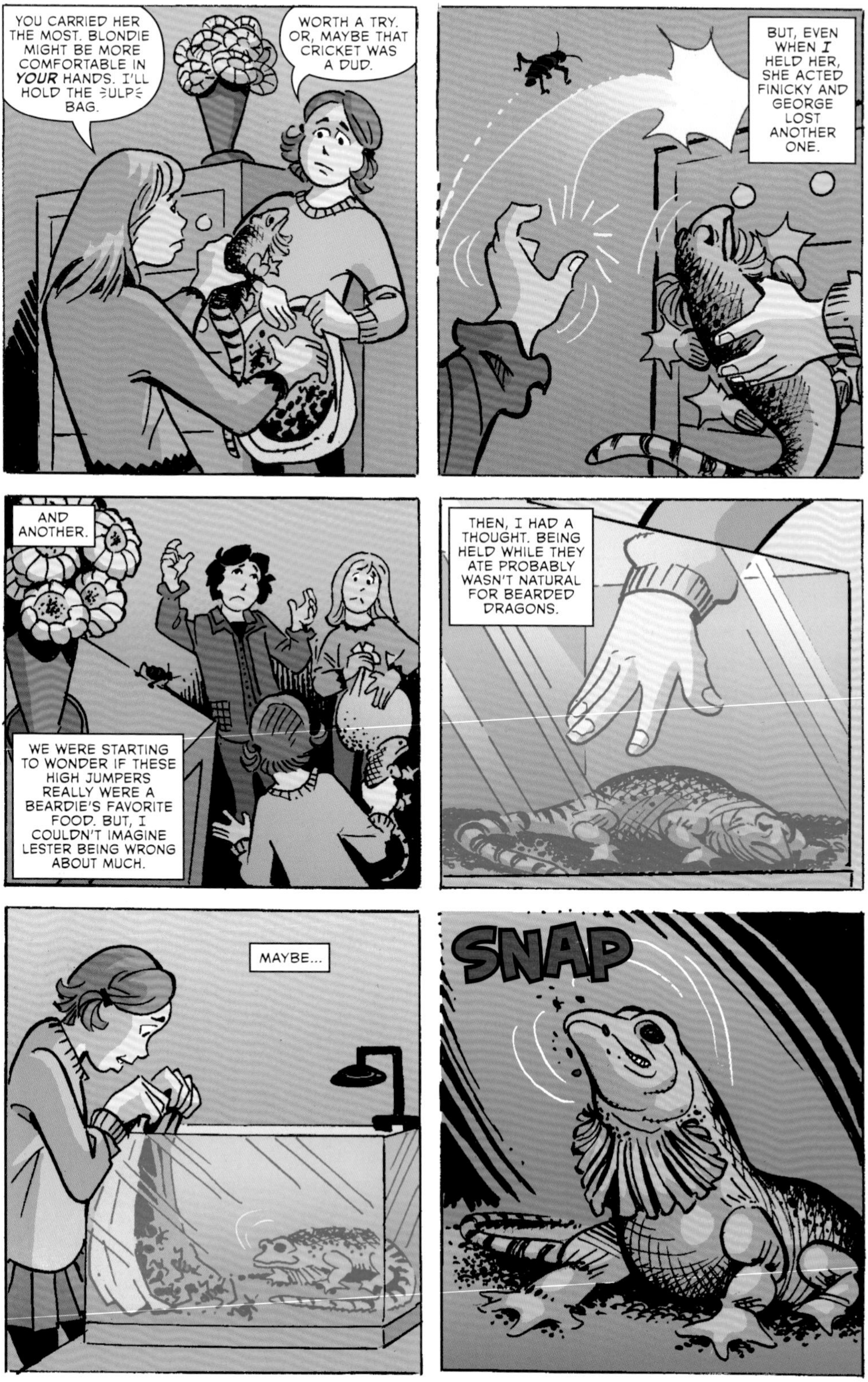
YOU CARRIED HER THE MOST. BLONDIE MIGHT BE MORE COMFORTABLE IN *YOUR* HANDS. I'LL HOLD THE ULP BAG.
WORTH A TRY. OR, MAYBE THAT CRICKET WAS A DUD.
BUT, EVEN WHEN *I* HELD HER, SHE ACTED FINICKY AND GEORGE LOST ANOTHER ONE.
AND ANOTHER.
WE WERE STARTING TO WONDER IF THESE HIGH JUMPERS REALLY WERE A BEARDIE'S FAVORITE FOOD. BUT, I COULDN'T IMAGINE LESTER BEING WRONG ABOUT MUCH.
THEN, I HAD A THOUGHT. BEING HELD WHILE THEY ATE PROBABLY WASN'T NATURAL FOR BEARDED DRAGONS.
MAYBE...
SNAP

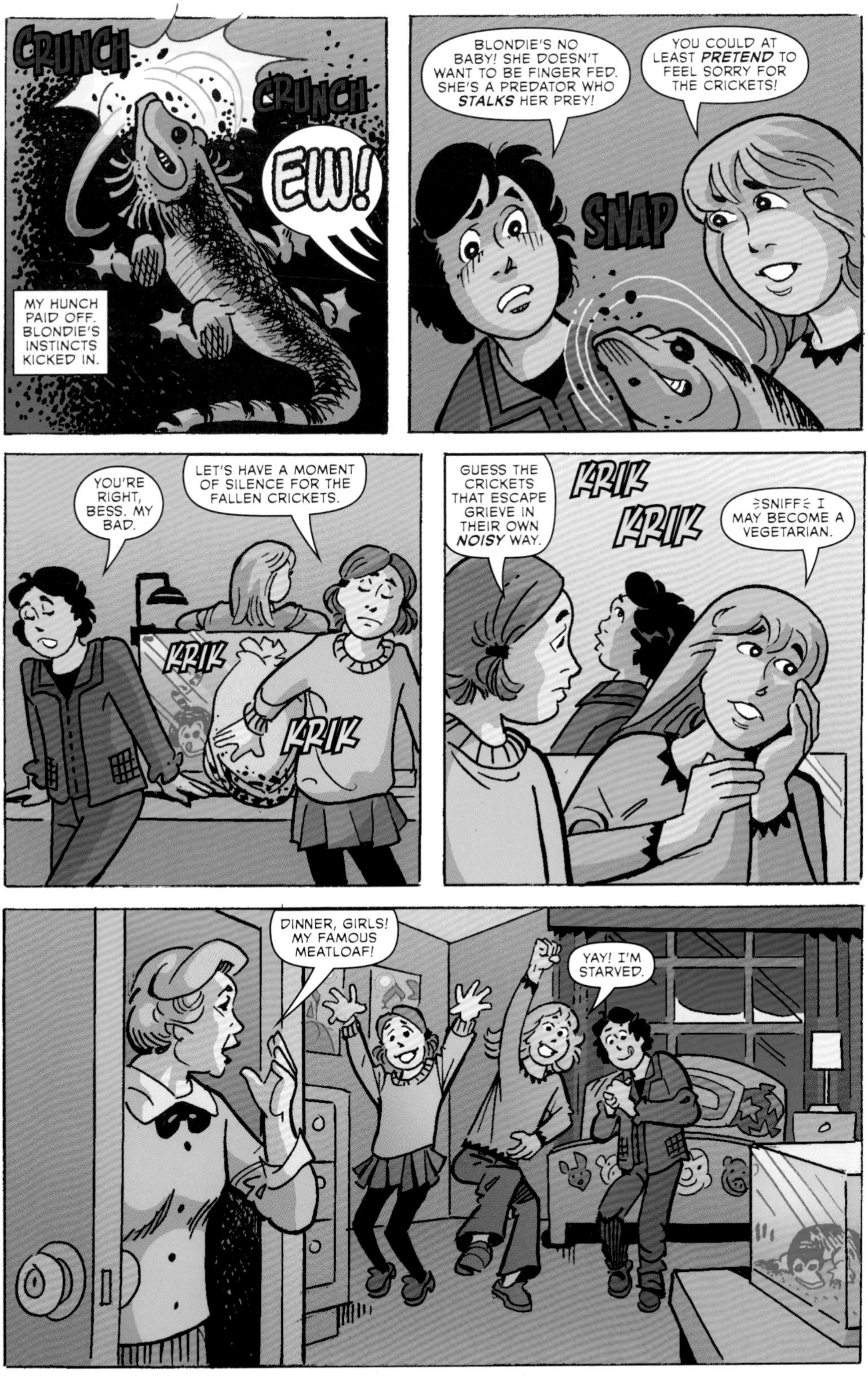
CRUNCH
CRUNCH
EW!
MY HUNCH PAID OFF. BLONDIE'S INSTINCTS KICKED IN.
BLONDIE'S NO BABY! SHE DOESN'T WANT TO BE FINGER FED. SHE'S A PREDATOR WHO STALKS HER PREY!
YOU COULD AT LEAST PRETEND TO FEEL SORRY FOR THE CRICKETS!
SNAP
YOU'RE RIGHT, BESS. MY BAD.
LET'S HAVE A MOMENT OF SILENCE FOR THE FALLEN CRICKETS.
KRIK
KRIK
GUESS THE CRICKETS THAT ESCAPE GRIEVE IN THEIR OWN NOISY WAY.
KRIK
KRIK
SNIFF I MAY BECOME A VEGETARIAN.
DINNER, GIRLS! MY FAMOUS MEATLOAF!
YAY! I'M STARVED.

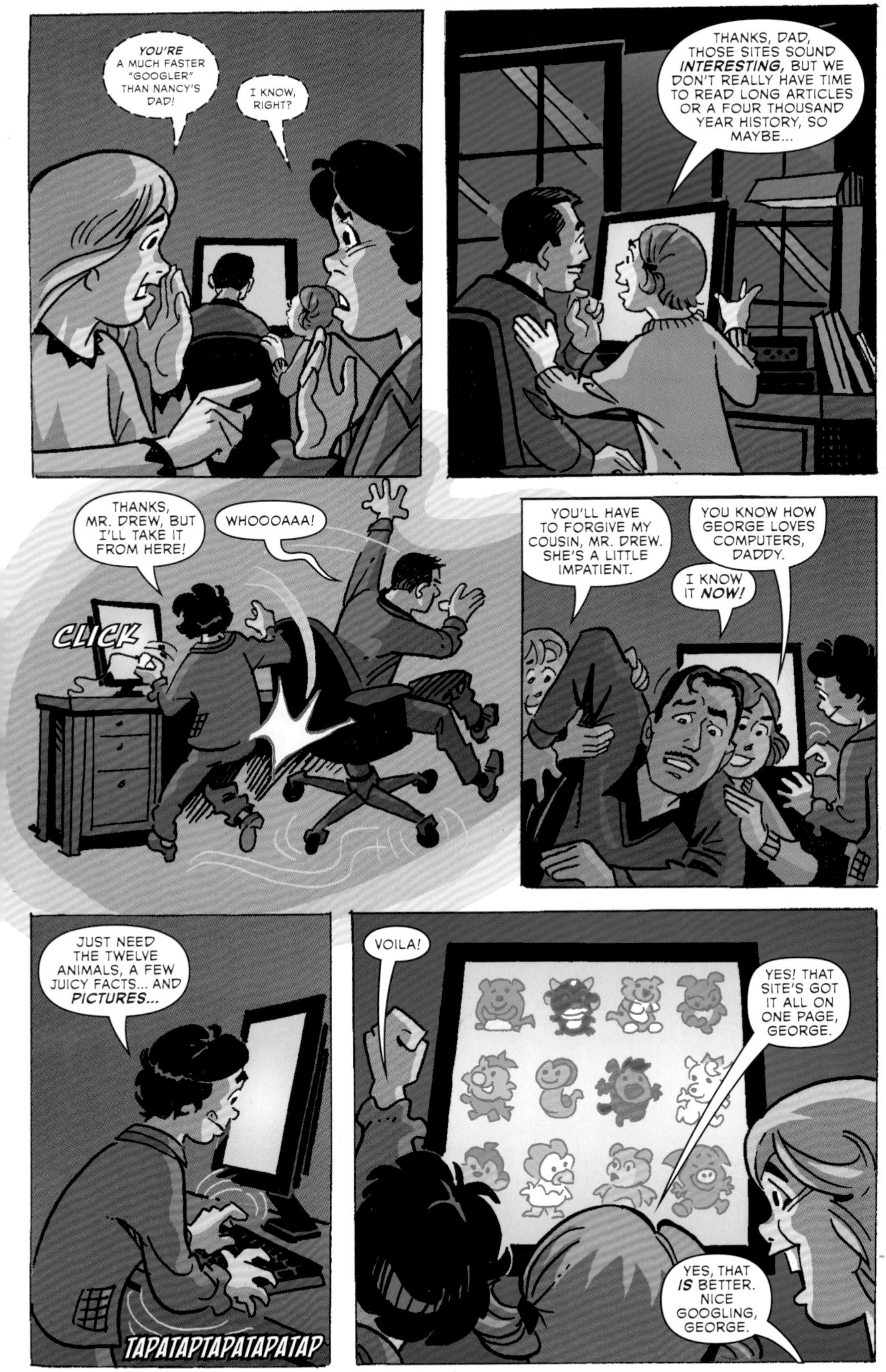
YOU'RE A MUCH FASTER "GOOGLER" THAN NANCY'S DAD!
I KNOW, RIGHT?
THANKS, DAD, THOSE SITES SOUND INTERESTING, BUT WE DON'T REALLY HAVE TIME TO READ LONG ARTICLES OR A FOUR THOUSAND YEAR HISTORY, SO MAYBE...
THANKS, MR. DREW, BUT I'LL TAKE IT FROM HERE!
WHOOOAAA!
CLICK
YOU'LL HAVE TO FORGIVE MY COUSIN, MR. DREW. SHE'S A LITTLE IMPATIENT.
YOU KNOW HOW GEORGE LOVES COMPUTERS, DADDY.
I KNOW IT NOW!
JUST NEED THE TWELVE ANIMALS, A FEW JUICY FACTS... AND PICTURES...
TAPATAPTAPATAPATAP
VOILA!
YES! THAT SITE'S GOT IT ALL ON ONE PAGE, GEORGE.
YES, THAT IS BETTER. NICE GOOGLING, GEORGE.

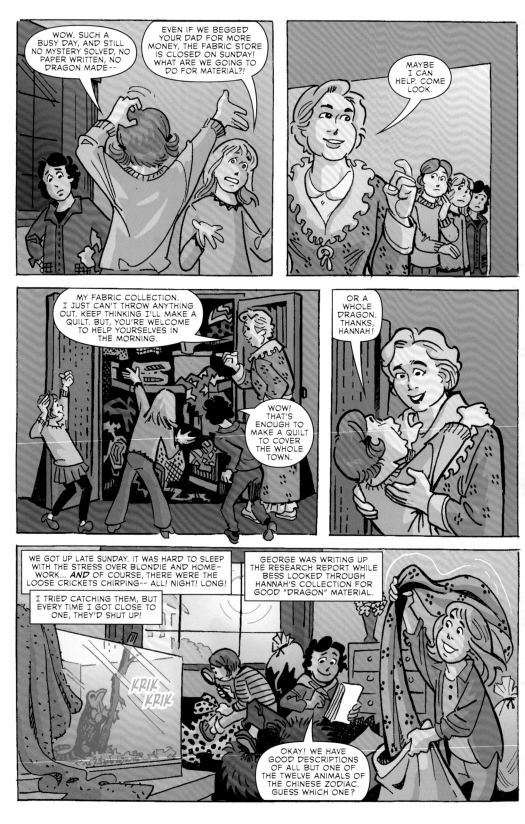

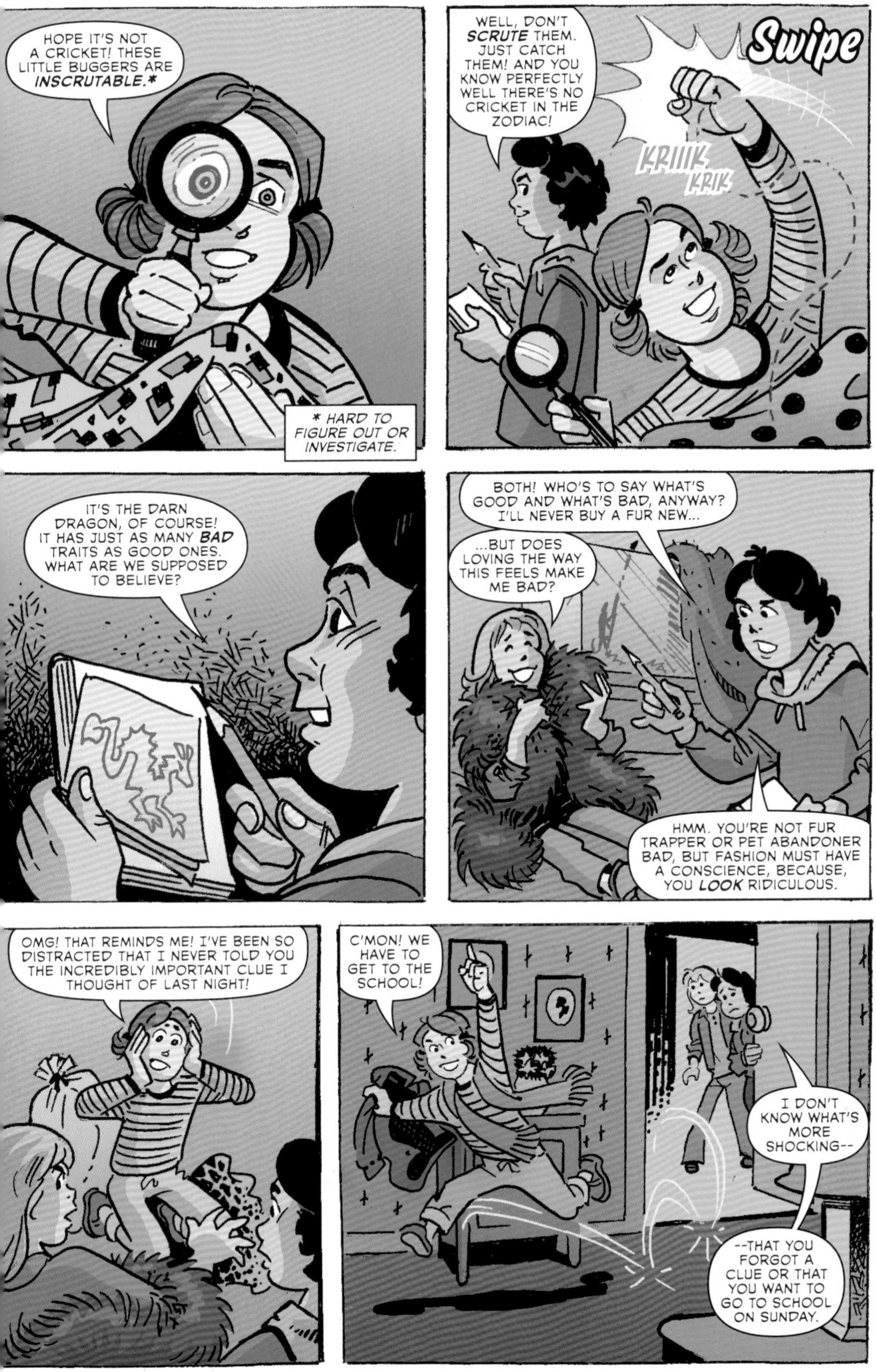
HOPE IT'S NOT A CRICKET! THESE LITTLE BUGGERS ARE *INSCRUTABLE.**
* HARD TO FIGURE OUT OR INVESTIGATE.
WELL, DON'T *SCRUTE* THEM. JUST CATCH THEM! AND YOU KNOW PERFECTLY WELL THERE'S NO CRICKET IN THE ZODIAC!
Swipe
KRIIIK
KRIK
IT'S THE DARN DRAGON, OF COURSE! IT HAS JUST AS MANY *BAD* TRAITS AS GOOD ONES. WHAT ARE WE SUPPOSED TO BELIEVE?
BOTH! WHO'S TO SAY WHAT'S GOOD AND WHAT'S BAD, ANYWAY? I'LL NEVER BUY A FUR NEW...
...BUT DOES LOVING THE WAY THIS FEELS MAKE ME BAD?
HMM. YOU'RE NOT FUR TRAPPER OR PET ABANDONER BAD, BUT FASHION MUST HAVE A CONSCIENCE, BECAUSE, YOU *LOOK* RIDICULOUS.
OMG! THAT REMINDS ME! I'VE BEEN SO DISTRACTED THAT I NEVER TOLD YOU THE INCREDIBLY IMPORTANT CLUE I THOUGHT OF LAST NIGHT!
C'MON! WE HAVE TO GET TO THE SCHOOL!
I DON'T KNOW WHAT'S MORE SHOCKING--
--THAT YOU FORGOT A CLUE OR THAT YOU WANT TO GO TO SCHOOL ON SUNDAY.

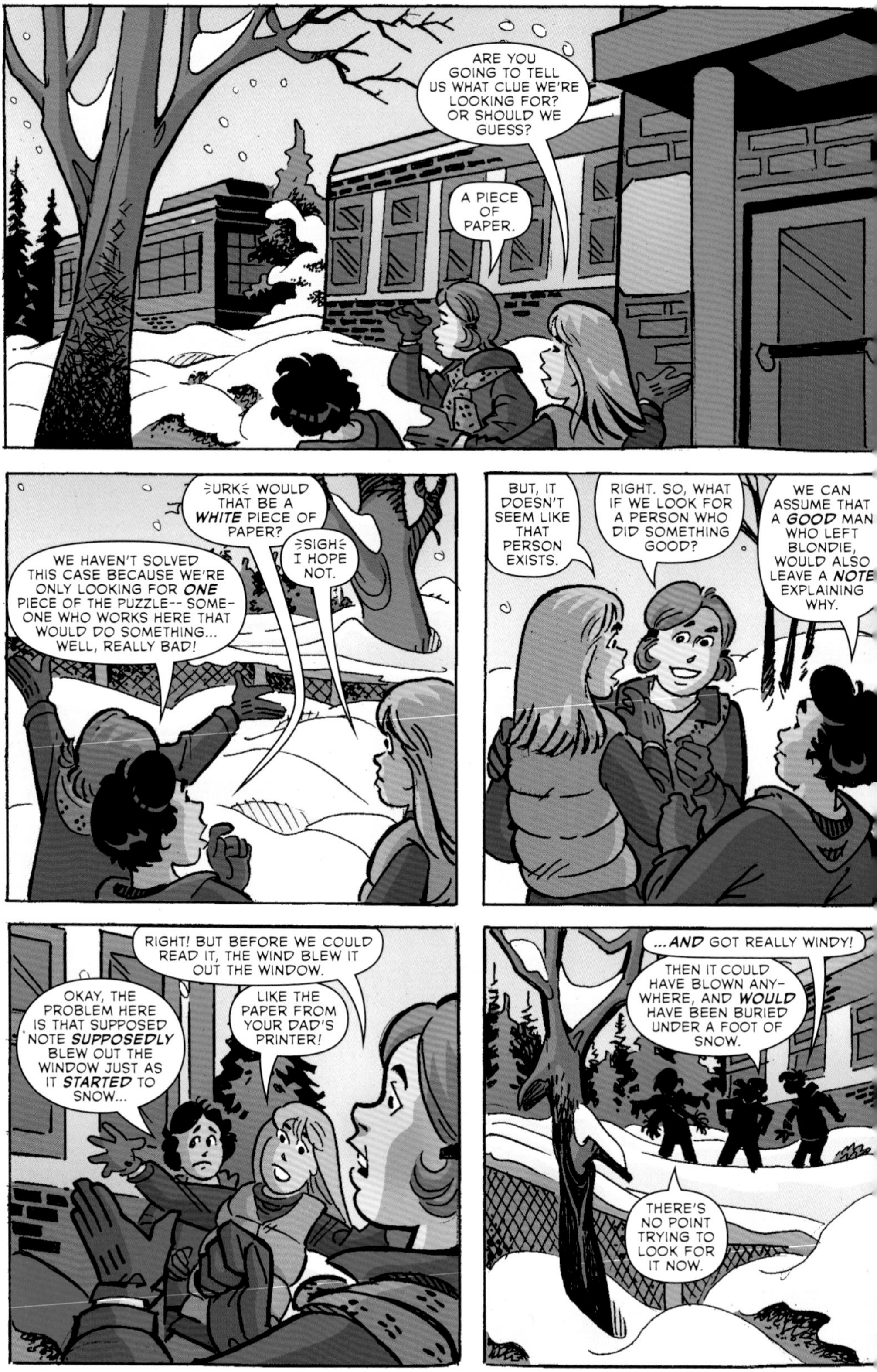
ARE YOU GOING TO TELL US WHAT CLUE WE'RE LOOKING FOR? OR SHOULD WE GUESS?
A PIECE OF PAPER.
=URK= WOULD THAT BE A *WHITE* PIECE OF PAPER?
=SIGH= I HOPE NOT.
WE HAVEN'T SOLVED THIS CASE BECAUSE WE'RE ONLY LOOKING FOR *ONE* PIECE OF THE PUZZLE-- SOMEONE WHO WORKS HERE THAT WOULD DO SOMETHING... WELL, REALLY BAD!
BUT, IT DOESN'T SEEM LIKE THAT PERSON EXISTS.
RIGHT. SO, WHAT IF WE LOOK FOR A PERSON WHO DID SOMETHING GOOD?
WE CAN ASSUME THAT A *GOOD* MAN WHO LEFT BLONDIE, WOULD ALSO LEAVE A *NOTE* EXPLAINING WHY.
RIGHT! BUT BEFORE WE COULD READ IT, THE WIND BLEW IT OUT THE WINDOW.
OKAY, THE PROBLEM HERE IS THAT SUPPOSED NOTE *SUPPOSEDLY* BLEW OUT THE WINDOW JUST AS IT *STARTED* TO SNOW...
LIKE THE PAPER FROM YOUR DAD'S PRINTER!
...AND GOT REALLY WINDY!
THEN IT COULD HAVE BLOWN ANYWHERE, AND *WOULD* HAVE BEEN BURIED UNDER A FOOT OF SNOW.
THERE'S NO POINT TRYING TO LOOK FOR IT NOW.

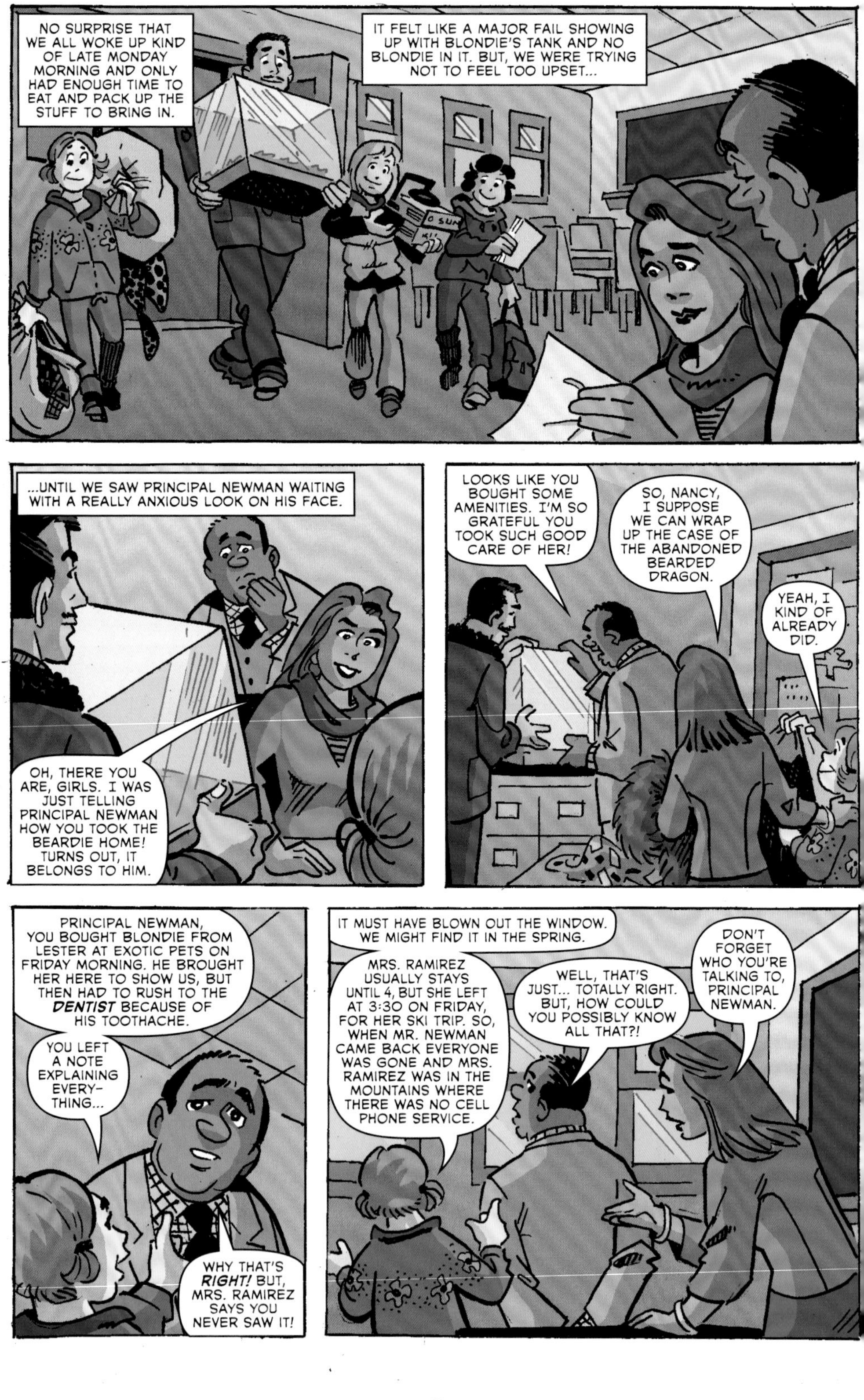
NO SURPRISE THAT WE ALL WOKE UP KIND OF LATE MONDAY MORNING AND ONLY HAD ENOUGH TIME TO EAT AND PACK UP THE STUFF TO BRING IN.
IT FELT LIKE A MAJOR FAIL SHOWING UP WITH BLONDIE'S TANK AND NO BLONDIE IN IT. BUT, WE WERE TRYING NOT TO FEEL TOO UPSET...
...UNTIL WE SAW PRINCIPAL NEWMAN WAITING WITH A REALLY ANXIOUS LOOK ON HIS FACE.
OH, THERE YOU ARE, GIRLS. I WAS JUST TELLING PRINCIPAL NEWMAN HOW YOU TOOK THE BEARDIE HOME! TURNS OUT, IT BELONGS TO HIM.
LOOKS LIKE YOU BOUGHT SOME AMENITIES. I'M SO GRATEFUL YOU TOOK SUCH GOOD CARE OF HER!
SO, NANCY, I SUPPOSE WE CAN WRAP UP THE CASE OF THE ABANDONED BEARDED DRAGON.
YEAH, I KIND OF ALREADY DID.
PRINCIPAL NEWMAN, YOU BOUGHT BLONDIE FROM LESTER AT EXOTIC PETS ON FRIDAY MORNING. HE BROUGHT HER HERE TO SHOW US, BUT THEN HAD TO RUSH TO THE *DENTIST* BECAUSE OF HIS TOOTHACHE.
YOU LEFT A NOTE EXPLAINING EVERY-THING...
WHY THAT'S *RIGHT!* BUT, MRS. RAMIREZ SAYS YOU NEVER SAW IT!
IT MUST HAVE BLOWN OUT THE WINDOW. WE MIGHT FIND IT IN THE SPRING.
MRS. RAMIREZ USUALLY STAYS UNTIL 4, BUT SHE LEFT AT 3:30 ON FRIDAY, FOR HER SKI TRIP. SO, WHEN MR. NEWMAN CAME BACK EVERYONE WAS GONE AND MRS. RAMIREZ WAS IN THE MOUNTAINS WHERE THERE WAS NO CELL PHONE SERVICE.
WELL, THAT'S JUST... TOTALLY RIGHT. BUT, HOW COULD YOU POSSIBLY KNOW ALL THAT?!
DON'T FORGET WHO YOU'RE TALKING TO, PRINCIPAL NEWMAN.

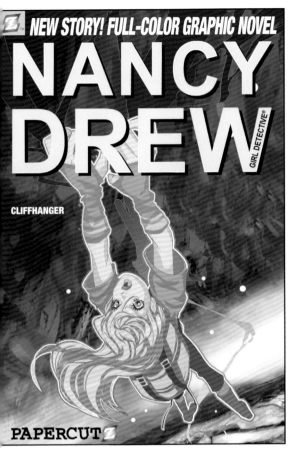

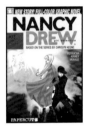

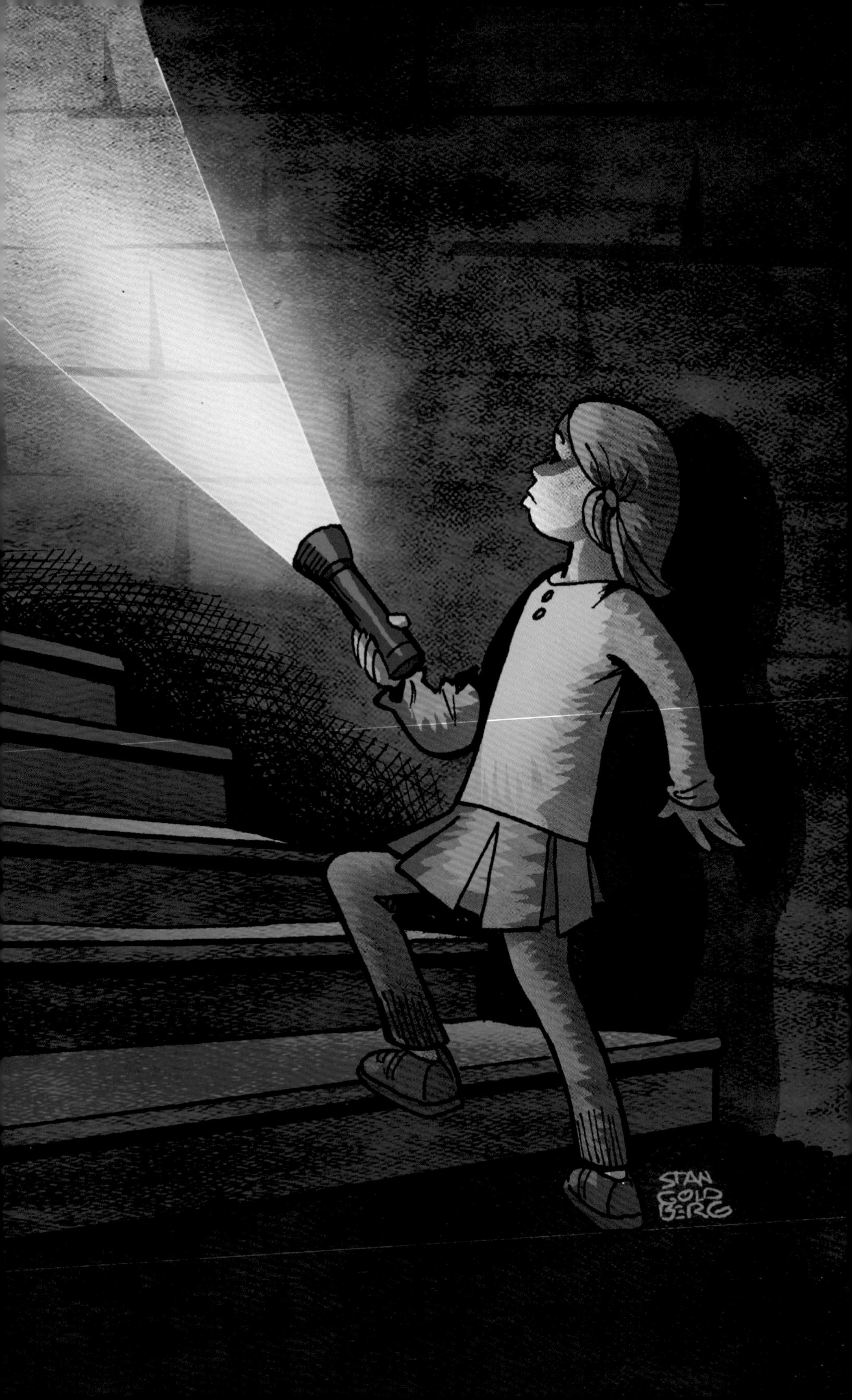
STAN GOLDBERG

WATCH OUT FOR PAPERCUTZ ™

Welcome to the totally thrilling third NANCY DREW AND THE CLUE CREW graphic novel from Papercutz, the perpetually perplexed and puzzled people dedicated to publishing great graphic novels for all ages. I'm Jim Salicrup, the Editor-in-Chief and magnifying glass maintainer, and I'm happy that you've picked up this Papercutz graphic novel.

We've got BIG NEWS for Nancy Drew fans! Due to popular demand, we'll soon be publishing another NANCY DREW title, this one featuring the 18 year old Nancy! So many of you have written to us asking where to find many of the out-of-print earlier NANCY DREW graphic novels by Stefan Petrucha (and later, Sarah Kinney) and Sho Murase (and a couple drawn by Vaughn Ross), that we realized it might just be a good idea to bring them back into print! Of course, many are still available directly from us via mail order or as ebooks, but now we have a new series that will be available in bookstores. We'll be calling it NANCY DREW DIARIES, and each volume will feature two complete graphic novels from the earlier series.

In the meantime, we just had to show you (on the opposite page) this beautiful bit of artwork, drawn by Stan Goldberg and colored by Laurie E. Smith, that was used on the free NANCY DREW AND THE CLUE CREW tote bags given away recently at the Book Expo: America. The bags were so popular they were all gone in a matter of hours! I don't even have one, but I think I know where Jesse Post, our Director of Marketing, may be hiding a few!

More BIG NEWS! If you're at all familiar with www.stardoll.com, then you already know what a super-cool website that is—especially if you're into fashion! Well, Papercutz has managed to sign a deal for us to create STARDOLL graphic novels, and they're like nothing you've ever seen before! In fact, we're offering a sneak preview of the first graphic novel, "Secrets & Dreams" on the following pages! What could possibly be better than that?

Even more BIG NEWS! Well, since I asked, I'll answer that the very next NANCY DREW AND THE CLUE CREW is really super-special! The title tells you everything you need to know, so be sure not to miss: NANCY DREW AND THE CLUE CREW #4 "A Girl Detective in Oz." (Hint: We're not talking about Nancy going to Australia!)

Thanks,

Jim

STAY IN TOUCH!

EMAIL: salicrup@papercutz.com
WEB: www.papercutz.com
TWITTER: @papercutzgn
FACEBOOK: PAPERCUTZGRAPHICNOVELS
SNAIL MAIL: Papercutz, 160 Broadway, Suite 700, East Wing, New York, NY 10038

stardoll™
Secrets & Dreams

by JayJay Jackson

Claire Leo

Fashion Style:
Casual, Fashion Forward
Dream:
To be a Fashion Designer

Ashley Archer

Fashion Style:
Feminine, Athletic
Dream:
To be a Fashion Business Manager

Kaya Reynard

Fashion Style:
Eclectic, Loves trying different styles
Dream:
To be an Interior Decorator

Sue-Ni MacDuffie

Fashion Style:
Asian inspired, Feminine, Pretty
Dream:
To be a Fashion Buyer

Ruby Zara

Fashion Style:
80's Vintage, Geek Chic
Dream:
Developing Fashion Technologies

To be continued in STARDOLL #1 "Secrets & Dreams," coming Fall 2013! And be sure to visit www.stardoll.com

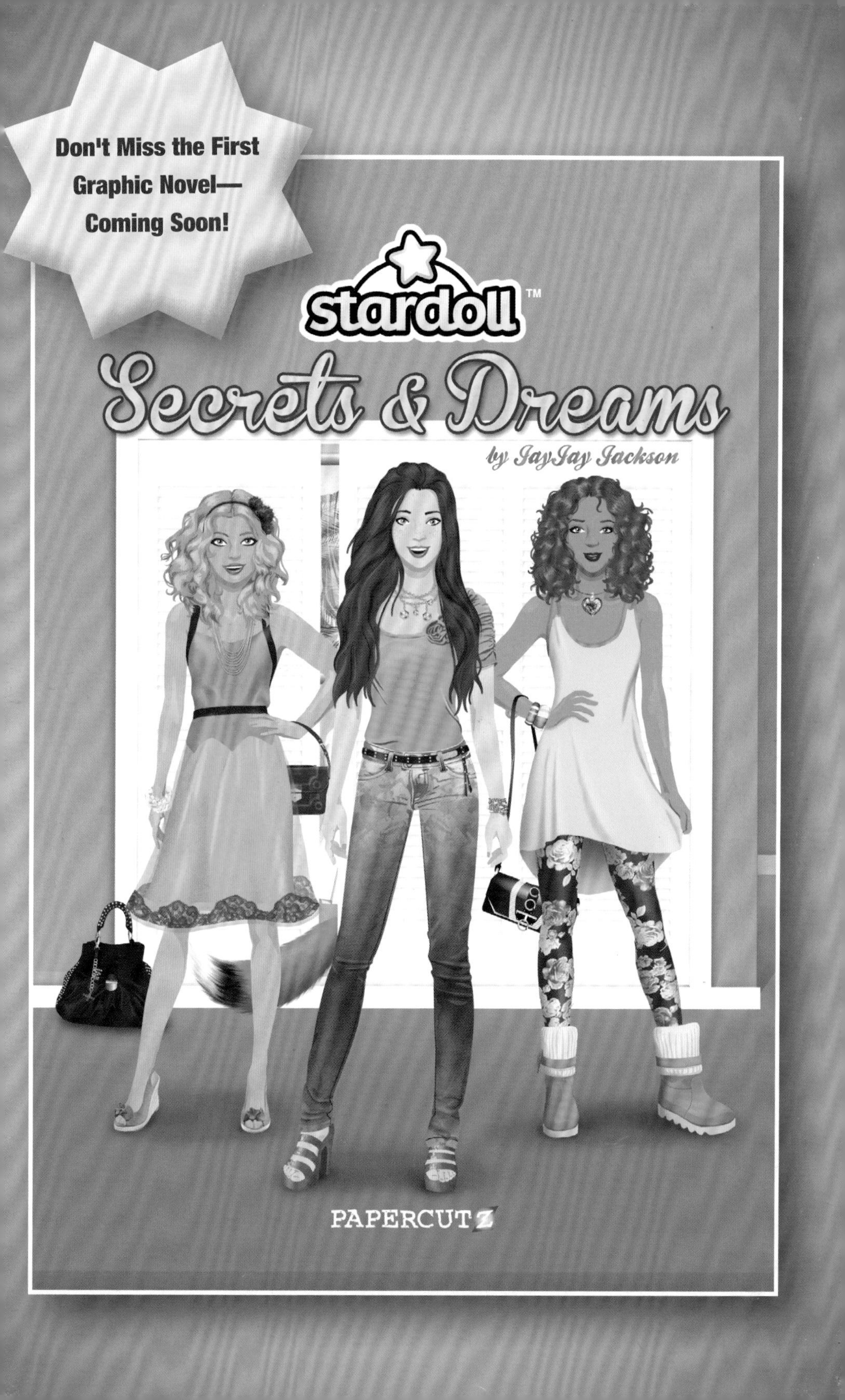
Don't Miss the First
Graphic Novel—
Coming Soon!
stardoll™
Secrets & Dreams
by JayJay Jackson
PAPERCUTZ

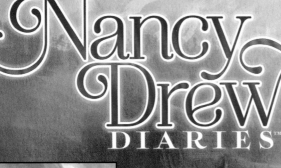
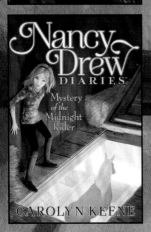

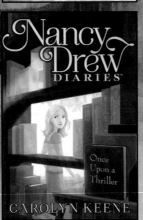
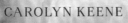

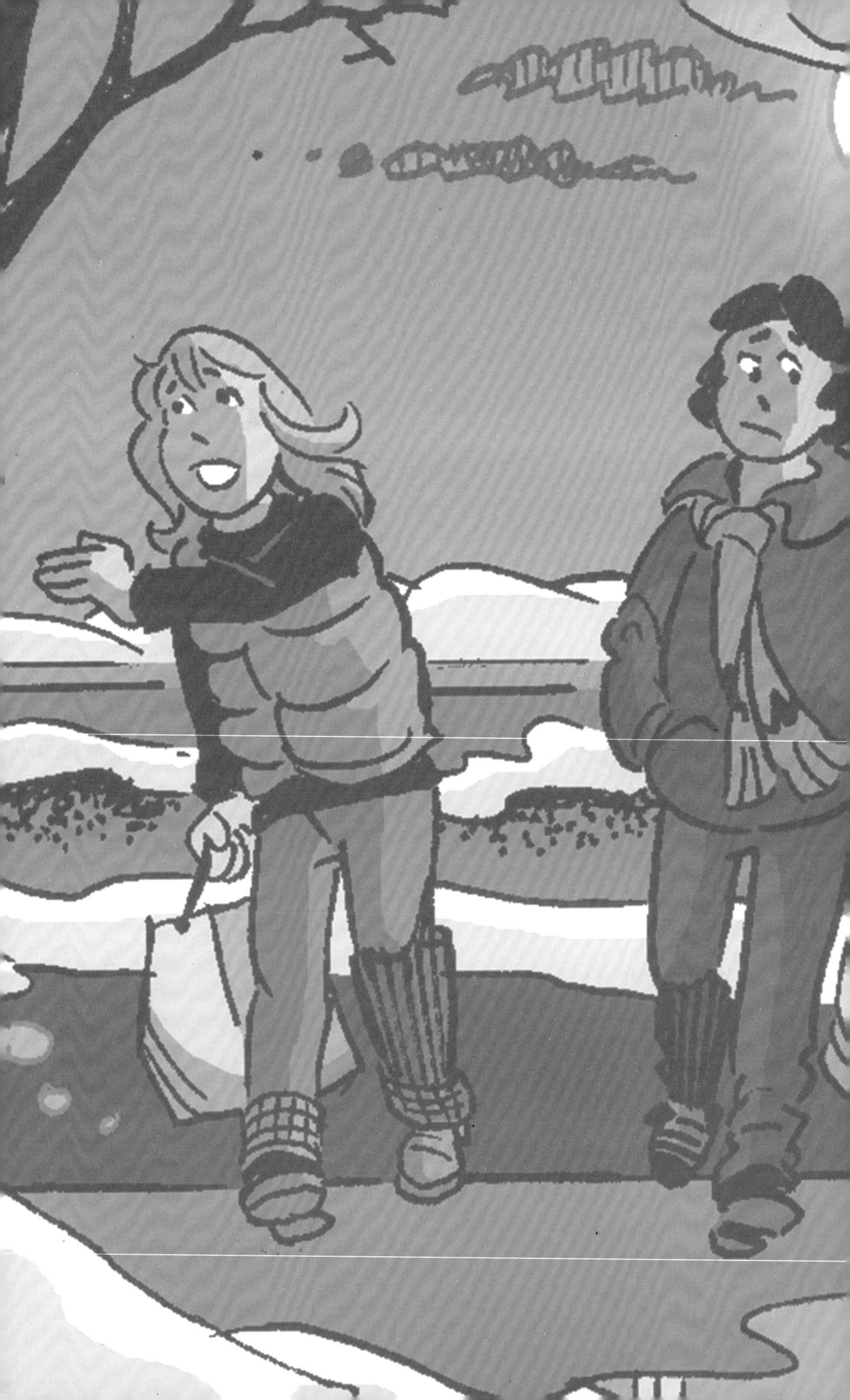